# Cat's Cradle

KURT VONNEGUT

PENGUIN BOOKS

PENGUIN ESSENTIALS

Published by the Penguin Group
Penguin Books Ltd, 80 Strand, London WC2R ORL, England
Penguin Group (USA) Inc., 375 Hudson Street, New York, New York 10014, USA
Penguin Group (Canada), 90 Eglinton Avenue East, Suite 700, Toronto, Ontario, Canada M4P 2Y3
(a division of Pearson Penguin Canada Inc.)
Penguin Ireland, 25 St Stephen's Green, Dublin 2, Ireland (a division of Penguin Books Ltd)
Penguin Group (Australia), 250 Camberwell Road, Camberwell, Victoria 3124, Australia
(a division of Pearson Australia Group Pty Ltd)
Penguin Books India Pvt Ltd, 11 Community Centre, Panchsheel Park,
New Delhi – 110 017, India
Penguin Group (NZ), 67 Apollo Drive, Rosedale, Auckland 0632, New Zealand
(a division of Pearson New Zealand Ltd)
Penguin Books (South Africa) (Pty) Ltd, 24 Sturdee Avenue,
Rosebank, Johannesburg 2196, South Africa

Penguin Books Ltd, Registered Offices: 80 Strand, London WC2R ORL, England

www.penguin.com

First published in the United States of America 1963
First published in Great Britain by Victor Gollancz Ltd 1963
First published in Penguin Books 1965
This Penguin Essentials edition published 2011

008

Printed in England by Clays Ltd, St Ives plc

Grateful acknowledgement is made to Mrs E. L. Masters for permission
to reprint 'Knowlt Hoheimer' from *Spoon River Anthology* by Edgar Lee Masters.
Copyright © Macmillan, 1914, 1915, 1942

ISBN: 978-0-241-95160-6

www.greenpenguin.co.uk

*For Kenneth Littauer, a man of*
*gallantry and taste*

Nothing in this book is true.

'Live by the *forma*★ that make you brave and kind and healthy and happy.'

*The Books of Bokonon.* 1:5

★Harmless untruths

## 1 *The Day the World Ended*

Call me Jonah. My parents did, or nearly did. They called me John.

Jonah – John – if I had been a Sam, I would have been a Jonah still – not because I have been unlucky for others, but because somebody or something has compelled me to be certain places at certain times, without fail. Conveyances and motives, both conventional and bizarre, have been provided. And, according to plan, at each appointed second, at each appointed place this Jonah was there.

Listen:

When I was a younger man – two wives ago, 250,000 cigarettes ago, 3,000 quarts of booze ago . . .

When I was a much younger man, I began to collect material for a book to be called *The Day the World Ended*.

The book was to be factual.

The book was to be an account of what important Americans had done on the day when the first atomic bomb was dropped on Hiroshima, Japan.

It was to be a Christian book. I was a Christian then.

I am a Bokononist now.

I would have been a Bokononist then, if there had been anyone to teach me the bittersweet lies of Bokonon. But Bokononism was unknown beyond the gravel beaches and coral knives that ring this little island in the Caribbean Sea, the Republic of San Lorenzo.

We Bokononists believe that humanity is organized into teams, teams that do God's Will without ever discovering what they are doing. Such a team is called a *karass* by Bokonon, and the instrument, the *kan-kan*, that brought me into my own particular *karass* was the book I never finished, the book to be called *The Day the World Ended*.

## 2 Nice, Nice, Very Nice

'If you find your life tangled up with somebody else's life for no very logical reasons,' writes Bokonon, 'that person may be a member of your *karass*.'

At another point in *The Books of Bokonon* he tells us, 'Man created the checkerboard; God created the *karass*.' By that he means that a *karass* ignores national, institutional, occupational, familial, and class boundaries.

It is as free-form as an amoeba.

In his 'Fifty-third Calypso' Bokonon invites us to sing along with him:

Oh, a sleeping drunkard
Up in Central Park,
And a lion-hunter
In the jungle dark,
And a Chinese dentist,
And a British queen –
All fit together
In the same machine.

Nice, nice, very nice;
Nice, nice, very nice;
Nice, nice, very nice –
So many different people
In the same device.

## 3 *Folly*

Nowhere does Bokonon warn against a person's trying to discover the limits of his *karass* and the nature of the work God Almighty has had it do. Bokonon simply observes that such investigations are bound to be incomplete.

In the autobiographical section of *The Books of Bokonon* he writes a parable on the folly of pretending to discover, to understand:

I once knew an Episcopalian lady in Newport, Rhode Island, who asked me to design and build a doghouse for her Great Dane. The lady claimed to understand God and His Ways of Working perfectly. She could not understand why anyone should be puzzled about what had been or about what was going to be.

And yet, when I showed her a blueprint of the doghouse I proposed to build, she said to me, 'I'm sorry, but I never could read one of those things.'

'Give it to your husband or your minister to pass on to God,' I said, 'and, when God finds a minute, I'm sure he'll explain this doghouse of mine in a way that even *you* can understand.'

She fired me. I shall never forget her. She believed that God liked people in sailboats much better than He liked people in motorboats. She could not bear to look at a worm. When she saw a worm, she screamed.

She was a fool, and so am I, and so is anyone who thinks he sees what God is Doing, [writes Bokonon].

## 4 *A Tentative Tangling of Tendrils*

Be that as it may, I intend in this book to include as many members of my *karass* as possible, and I mean to examine all strong hints as to what on Earth we, collectively, have been up to.

I do not intend that this book be a tract on behalf of Bokononism. I should like to offer a Bokononist warning about it, however. The first sentence in *The Books of Bokonon* is this:

'All of the true things I am about to tell you are shameless lies.'

My Bokononist warning is this:

Anyone unable to understand how a useful religion can be founded on lies will not understand this book either.

So be it.

About my *karass*, then.

It surely includes the three children of Dr Felix Hoenikker, one of the so-called 'Fathers' of the first atomic bomb. Dr Hoenikker himself was no doubt a member of my *karass*, though he was dead before my *sinookas*, the tendrils of my life, began to tangle with those of his children.

The first of his heirs to be touched by my *sinookas* was Newton Hoenikker, the youngest of his three children, the younger of his two sons. I learned from the publication of my fraternity, the *Delta Upsilon Quarterly*, that Newton Hoenikker, son of the Nobel Prize physicist, Felix Hoenikker, had been pledged by my chapter, the Cornell Chapter.

So I wrote this letter to Newt:

'Dear Mr Hoenikker:

'Or should I say, Dear *Brother* Hoenikker?

'I am a Cornell DU now making my living as a free-lance writer. I am gathering material for a book relating to the first atomic bomb. Its contents will be limited to events that took place on 6 August, 1945, the day the bomb was dropped on Hiroshima.

'Since your late father is generally recognized as having been one of the chief creators of the bomb, I would very much appreciate any anecdotes you might care to give me of life in your father's house on the day the bomb was dropped.

'I am sorry to say that I don't know as much about your illustrious family as I should, and so don't know whether you have brothers and sisters. If you do have brothers and sisters, I should like very much to have their addresses so that I can send similar requests to them.

'I realize that you were very young when the bomb was dropped, which is all to the good. My book is going to emphasize the *human* rather than the *technical* side of the bomb, so recollections of the day through the eyes of a "Baby", if you'll pardon the expression, would fit in perfectly.

'You don't have to worry about style and form. Leave all that to me. Just give me the bare bones of your story.

'I will, of course, submit the final version to you for your approval prior to publication.

'Fraternally yours – '

## 5  *Letter from a Pre-med*

To which Newt replied:

'I am sorry to be so long about answering your letter. That sounds like a very interesting book you are doing. I was so young when the bomb was dropped that I don't think I'm going to be much help. You should really ask my brother and sister, who are both older than I am. My sister is Mrs Harrison C. Conners, 4918 North Meridian Street, Indianapolis, Indiana. That is my home address, too, now. I think she will be glad to help you. Nobody knows where my brother Frank is. He disappeared right after Father's funeral two years ago, and nobody has heard from him since. For all we know, he may be dead now.

'I was only six years old when they dropped the atomic bomb on Hiroshima, so anything I remember about that day other people have helped me to remember.

'I remember I was playing on the living-room carpet outside my father's study door in Ilium, New York. The door was open, and I could see my father. He was wearing pyjamas and a bathrobe. He was smoking a cigar. He was playing with a loop of string. Father was staying home from the laboratory in his pyjamas all day that day. He stayed home whenever he wanted to.

'Father, as you probably know, spent practically his whole professional life working for the Research Laboratory of the General Forge and Foundry Company in Ilium. When the Manhattan Project came along, the bomb project, Father wouldn't leave Ilium to work on it. He said he wouldn't work on it at all unless they let him work where he wanted to work. A lot of the time that meant at home. The only place he liked to go, outside of Ilium, was our cottage on Cape Cod. Cape

Cod was where he died. He died on a Christmas Eve. You probably know that, too.

'Anyway, I was playing on the carpet outside his study on the day of the bomb. My sister Angela tells me I used to play with little toy trucks for hours, making motor sounds, going "burton, burton, burton" all the time. So I guess I was going "burton, burton, burton" on the day of the bomb; and Father was in his study, playing with a loop of string.

'It so happens I know where the string he was playing with came from. Maybe you can use it somewhere in your book. Father took the string from around the manuscript of a novel that a man in prison had sent him. The novel was about the end of the world in the year 2000, and the name of the book was *2000 A.D.* It told about how mad scientists made a terrific bomb that wiped out the whole world. There was a big sex orgy when everybody knew that the world was going to end, and then Jesus Christ Himself appeared ten seconds before the bomb went off. The name of the author was Marvin Sharpe Holderness, and he told Father in a covering letter that he was in prison for killing his own brother. He sent the manuscript to Father because he couldn't figure out what kind of explosives to put in the bomb. He thought maybe Father could make suggestions.

'I don't mean to tell you I read the book when I was six. We had it around the house for years. My brother Frank made it his personal property, on account of the dirty parts. Frank kept it hidden in what he called his "wall safe" in his bedroom. Actually, it wasn't a safe but just an old stove flue with a tin lid. Frank and I must have read the orgy part a thousand times when we were kids. We had it for years, and then my sister Angela found it. She read it and said it was nothing but a piece of dirty rotten filth. She burned it up, and the string with it. She was a mother to Frank and me, because our real mother died when I was born.

'My father never read the book, I'm pretty sure. I don't think he ever read a novel or even a short story in his whole life, or at least not since he was a little boy. He didn't read his mail or magazines or newspapers, either. I suppose he read a lot of technical journals, but to tell you the truth, I can't remember my father reading anything.

'As I say, all he wanted from that manuscript was the string. That was the way he was. Nobody could predict what he was going to be interested in next. On the day of the bomb it was string.

'Have you ever read the speech he made when he accepted the Nobel Prize? This is the whole speech: "Ladies and Gentlemen. I stand before you now because I never stopped dawdling like an eight-year-old on a spring morning on his way to school. Anything can make me stop and look and wonder, and sometimes learn. I am a very happy man. Thank you."

'Anyway, Father looked at that loop of string for a while, and then his fingers started playing with it. His fingers made the string figure called a "cat's cradle". I don't know where Father learned how to do that. From *his* father, maybe. His father was a tailor, you know, so there must have been thread and string around all the time when Father was a boy.

'Making that cat's cradle was the closest I ever saw my father come to playing what anybody else would call a game. He had no use at all for tricks and games and rules that other people made up. In a scrapbook my sister Angela used to keep up, there was a clipping from *Time* magazine where somebody asked Father what games he played for relaxation, and he said, "Why should I bother with made-up games when there are so many real ones going on?"

'He must have surprised himself when he made a cat's cradle out of the string, and maybe it reminded him of his own childhood. He all of a sudden came out of his study and did something he'd never done before. He tried to play with me. Not only had he never played with me before; he had hardly ever even spoken to me.

'But he went down on his knees on the carpet next to me, and he showed me his teeth, and he waved that tangle of string in my face. "See? See? See?" he asked. "Cat's cradle. See the cat's cradle? See where the nice pussycat sleeps? Miaow. Miaow."

'His pores looked as big as craters on the moon. His ears and nostrils were stuffed with hair. Cigar smoke made him smell like the mouth of Hell. So close up, my father was the ugliest thing I had ever seen. I dream about it all the time.

'And then he sang. "Rockabye catsy, in the tree top", he sang, "when the wind blows, the cray-dull will rock. If the bough breaks, the cray-dull will fall. Down will come cray-dull, catsy, and all."

'I burst into tears. I jumped up and I ran out of the house as fast as I could go.

'I have to sign off here. It's after two in the morning. My room-mate just woke up and complained about the noise from the typewriter.'

## 6 Bug Fights

Newt resumed his letter the next morning. He resumed it as follows:

'Next morning. Here I go again, fresh as a daisy after eight hours of sleep. The fraternity house is very quiet now. Everybody is in class but me. I'm a very privileged character. I don't have to go to class any more. I was flunked out last week. I was a pre-med. They were right to flunk me out. I would have made a lousy doctor.

'After I finish this letter, I think I'll go to a movie. Or if the sun comes out, maybe I'll go for a walk through one of the gorges. Aren't the gorges beautiful? This year, two girls jumped into one holding hands. They didn't get into the sorority they wanted. They wanted Tri-Delt.

'But back to 6 August, 1945. My sister Angela has told me many times that I really hurt my father that day when I wouldn't admire the cat's cradle, when I wouldn't stay there on the carpet with my father and listen to him sing. Maybe I did hurt him, but I don't think I could have hurt him much. He was one of the best-protected human beings who ever lived. People couldn't get at him because he just wasn't interested in people. I remember one time, about a year before he died, I tried to get him to tell me something about my mother. He couldn't remember anything about her.

'Did you ever hear the famous story about breakfast on the day Mother and Father were leaving for Sweden to accept the Nobel Prize? It was in *The Saturday Evening Post* one time. Mother cooked a big breakfast. And then, when she cleared off the table, she found a quarter and a dime and three pennies by Father's coffee cup. He'd tipped her.

'After wounding my father so terribly, if that's what I did, I ran out into the yard. I didn't know where I was going until I found my brother Frank under a big spiraea bush. Frank was twelve then, and I wasn't surprised to find him under there. He spent a lot of time under there on hot days. Just like a dog, he'd make a hollow in the cool earth all around the roots. And you never could tell what Frank would have under the bush with him. One time he had a dirty book. Another time he had a bottle of cooking sherry. On the day they dropped the bomb Frank had a tablespoon and a Mason jar. What he was doing was spooning different kinds of bugs into the jar and making them fight.

'The bug fight was so interesting that I stopped crying right away – forgot all about the old man. I can't remember what all Frank had fighting in the jar that day, but I can remember other bug fights we staged later on: one stag beetle against a hundred red ants, one centipede against three spiders, red ants against black ants. They won't fight unless you keep shaking the jar. And that's what Frank was doing, shaking, shaking the jar.

'After a while Angela came looking for me. She lifted up one side of the bush and said, "So there you are!" She asked Frank what he thought he was doing, and he said, "Experimenting." That's what Frank always used to say when people asked him what he thought he was doing. He always said, "Experimenting."

'Angela was twenty-two then. She had been the real head of the family since she was sixteen, since Mother died, since I was born. She used to talk about how she had three children – me, Frank, and Father. She wasn't exaggerating, either. I can remember cold mornings when Frank, Father, and I would be all in a line in the front hall, and Angela would be bundling us up, treating us exactly the same. Only I was going to kindergarten; Frank was going to junior high; and Father was going to work on the atom bomb. I remember one morning like that when the oil burner had quit, the pipes were frozen, and the car wouldn't start. We all sat there in the car while Angela kept pushing the starter until the battery was dead. And then Father spoke up. You know what he said? He said, "I wonder about turtles." "What do you wonder about turtles?" Angela asked him. "When they pull in their heads," he said, "do their spines buckle or contract?"

'Angela was one of the unsung heroines of the atom bomb, incidentally, and I don't think the story has ever been told. Maybe you can use it. After the turtle incident, Father got so interested in turtles that he stopped working on the atom bomb.

Some people from the Manhattan Project finally came out to the house to ask Angela what to do. She told them to take away Father's turtles. So one night they went into his laboratory and stole the turtles and the aquarium. Father never said a word about the disappearance of the turtles. He just came to work the next day and looked for things to play with and think about, and everything there was to play with and think about had something to do with the bomb.

'When Angela got me out from under the bush, she asked me what had happened between Father and me. I just kept saying over and over again how ugly he was, how much I hated him. So she slapped me. "How dare you say that about your father?" she said. "He's one of the greatest men who ever lived! He won the war today! Do you realize that? He won the war!" She slapped me again.

'I don't blame Angela for slapping me. Father was all she had. She didn't have any boy friends. She didn't have any friends at all. She had only one hobby. She played the clarinet.

'I told her again how much I hated my father; she slapped me again; and then Frank came out from under the bush and punched her in the stomach. It hurt her something awful. She fell down and she rolled around. When she got her wind back, she cried and she yelled for Father.

' "He won't come," Frank said, and he laughed at her. Frank was right. Father stuck his head out a window, and he looked at Angela and me rolling on the ground, bawling, and Frank standing over us, laughing. The old man pulled his head indoors again, and never even asked later what all the fuss had been about. People weren't his speciality.

'Will that do? Is that any help to your book? Of course, you've really tied me down, asking me to stick to the day of the bomb. There are lots of other good anecdotes about the bomb and Father, from other days. For instance, do you know the story about Father on the day they first tested a bomb out at Alamogordo? After the thing went off, after it was a sure thing that America could wipe out a city with just one bomb, a scientist turned to Father and said, "Science has now known sin." And do you know what Father said? He said, "What is sin?"

'All the best,
'Newton Hoenikker'

## 7  *The Illustrious Hoenikkers*

Newt added these three postscripts to his letter:

'P.S. I can't sign myself "fraternally yours" because they won't let me be your brother on account of my grades. I was only a pledge, and now they are going to take even that away from me.

'P.P.S. You call our family "illustrious", and I think you would maybe be making a mistake if you called it that in your book. I am a midget, for instance – four feet tall. And the last we heard of my brother Frank, he was wanted by the Florida police, the F.B.I., and the Treasury Department for running stolen cars to Cuba on war-surplus L.S.T.'s. So I'm pretty sure "illustrious" isn't quite the word you're after. "Glamorous" is probably closer to the truth.

'P.P.P.S. Twenty-four hours later. I have re-read this letter and I can see where somebody might get the impression that I don't do anything but sit around and remember sad things and pity myself. Actually, I am a very lucky person and I know it. I am about to marry a wonderful little girl. There is love enough in this world for everybody, if people will just look. I am proof of that.'

## 8 *Newt's Thing with Zinka*

Newt did not tell me who his girl friend was. But about two weeks after he wrote to me everybody in the country knew that her name was Zinka – plain Zinka. Apparently she didn't have a last name.

Zinka was a Ukrainian midget, a dancer with the Borzoi Dance Company. As it happened, Newt saw a performance by that company in Indianapolis, before he went to Cornell. And then the company danced at Cornell. When the Cornell performance was over, little Newt was outside the stage door with a dozen long-stemmed American Beauty roses.

The newspapers picked up the story when little Zinka asked for political asylum in the United States, and then she and little Newt disappeared.

One week after that, little Zinka presented herself at the Russian Embassy. She said Americans were too materialistic. She said she wanted to go back home.

Newt took shelter in his sister's house in Indianapolis. He gave one brief statement to the press. 'It was a private matter,' he said. 'It was an affair of the heart. I have no regrets. What happened is nobody's business but Zinka's and my own.'

One enterprising American reporter in Moscow, making inquiries about Zinka among dance people there, made the unkind discovery that Zinka was not, as she claimed, only twenty-three years old.

She was forty-two – old enough to be Newt's mother.

## 9 *Vice-president in Charge of Volcanoes*

I loafed on my book about the day of the bomb.

About a year later, two days before Christmas, another story carried me through Ilium, New York, where Dr Felix Hoenikker had done most of his work; where little Newt, Frank, and Angela had spent their formative years.

I stopped off in Ilium to see what I could see.

There were no live Hoenikkers left in Ilium, but there were plenty of people who claimed to have known well the old man and his three peculiar children.

I made an appointment with Dr Asa Breed, Vice-president in charge of the Research Laboratory of the General Forge and Foundry Company. I suppose Dr Breed was a member of my *karass*, too, though he took a dislike to me almost immediately.

'Likes and dislikes have nothing to do with it,' says Bokonon – an easy warning to forget.

'I understand you were Dr Hoenikker's supervisor during most of his professional life,' I said to Dr Breed on the telephone.

'On paper,' he said.

'I don't understand,' I said.

'If I actually supervised Felix,' he said, 'then I'm ready now to take charge of volcanoes, the tides, and the migrations of birds and lemmings. The man was a force of nature no mortal could possibly control.'

## 10  Secret Agent X-9

Dr Breed made an appointment for me for early the next morning. He would pick me up at my hotel on his way to work, he said, thus simplifying my entry into the heavily-guarded Research Laboratory.

So I had a night to kill in Ilium. I was already in the beginning and end of night life in Ilium, the Del Prado Hotel. Its bar, the Cape Cod Room, was a hangout for whores.

As it happened – 'as it was *meant* to happen', Bokonon would say – the whore next to me at the bar and the bartender serving me had both gone to high school with Franklin Hoenikker, the bug tormentor, the middle child, the missing son.

The whore, who said her name was Sandra, offered me delights unobtainable outside of Place Pigalle and Port Said. I said I wasn't interested, and she was bright enough to say that she wasn't really interested either. As things turned out, we had both overestimated our apathies, but not by much.

Before we took the measure of each other's passions, how-ever, we talked about Frank Hoenikker, and we talked about the old man, and we talked a little about Asa Breed, and we talked about the General Forge and Foundry Company, and we talked about the Pope and birth control, about Hitler and the Jews. We talked about phonies. We talked about truth. We talked about gangsters; we talked about business. We talked about the nice poor people who went to the electric chair; and we talked about the rich bastards who didn't. We talked about religious people who had perversions. We talked about a lot of things.

We got drunk.

The bartender was very nice to Sandra. He liked her. He respected her. He told me that Sandra had been chairman of the Class Colours Committee at Ilium High. Every class, he explained, got to pick distinctive colours for itself in its junior year, and then it got to wear those colours with pride.

'What colours did you pick?' I asked.

'Orange and black.'

'Those are good colours.'

'I thought so.'

'Was Franklin Hoenikker on the Class Colours Committee, too?'

'He wasn't on anything,' said Sandra scornfully. 'He never got on any committee, never played any game, never took any girl out. I don't think he ever even talked to a girl. We used to call him Secret Agent X-9.'

'X-9?'

'You know – he was always acting like he was on his way between two secret places; couldn't ever talk to anybody.'

'Maybe he really *did* have a very rich secret life,' I suggested.

'Nah.'

'Nah,' sneered the bartender. 'He was just one of those kids who made model airplaines and jerked off all the time.'

## 11 *Protein*

'He was supposed to be our commencement speaker,' said Sandra.

'Who was?' I asked.

'Dr Hoenikker – the old man.'

'What did he say?'

'He didn't show up.'

'So you didn't get a commencement address?'

'Oh, we got one. Dr Breed, the one you're gonna see

tomorrow, he showed up, all out of breath, and he gave some kind of talk.'

'What did he say?'

'He said he hoped a lot of us would have careers in science,' she said. She didn't see anything funny in that. She was remembering a lesson that had impressed her. She was repeating it gropingly, dutifully. 'He said, the trouble with the world was . . .'

She had to stop and think.

'The trouble with the world was,' she continued hesitatingly, 'that people were still superstitious instead of scientific. He said if everybody would study science more, there wouldn't be all the trouble there was.'

'He said science was going to discover the basic secret of life some day,' the bartender put in. He scratched his head and frowned. 'Didn't I read in the paper the other day where they'd finally found out what it was?'

'I missed that,' I murmured.

'I saw that,' said Sandra. 'About two days ago.'

'That's right,' said the bartender.

'What *is* the secret of life?' I asked.

'I forget,' said Sandra.

'Protein,' the bartender declared. 'They found out something about protein.'

'Yeah,' said Sandra, 'that's it.'

## 12 *End of the World Delight*

An older bartender came over to join in our conversation in the Cape Cod Room of the Del Prado. When he heard that I was writing a book about the day of the bomb, he told me what the day had been like for him, what the day had been like in the very bar in which we sat. He had a W. C. Fields twang and a nose like a prize strawberry.

'It wasn't the Cape Cod Room then,' he said. 'We didn't have all these fugging nets and seashells around. It was called the Navajo Tepee in those days. Had Indian blankets and cow skulls on the walls. Had little tom-toms on the tables. People were supposed to beat on the tom-toms when they wanted service. They tried to get me to wear a war bonnet, but I wouldn't do it. Real Navajo Indian came in here one day; told me Navajos didn't live in tepees. "That's a fugging shame," I told him. Before that it was the Pompeii Room, with busted plaster all over the place; but no matter what they call the room, they never change the fugging light fixtures. Never change the fugging people who come in or the fugging town outside, either. The day they dropped Hoenikker's fugging bomb on the Japanese a bum came in and tried to scrounge a drink. He wanted me to give him a drink on account of the world was coming to an end. So I mixed him an "End of the World Delight". I gave him about a half-pint of crème de menthe in a hollowed-out pineapple, with whipped cream and a cherry on top. "There, you pitiful son of a bitch," I said to him, "don't ever say I never did anything for you." Another guy came in, and he said he was quitting his job at the Research Laboratory; said anything a scientist worked on was sure to wind up as a weapon, one way or another. Said he didn't want to help politicians with their fugging wars any more. Name was Breed. I asked him if he was any relation to the boss of the fugging Research Laboratory. He said he fugging well was. Said he was the boss of the Research Laboratory's fugging son.'

Cat's Cradle

## 13  The Jumping-off Place

Ah, God, what an ugly city Ilium is!

'Ah, God,' says Bokonon, 'what an ugly city every city is!'

Sleet was falling through a motionless blanket of smog. It was early morning. I was riding in the Lincoln sedan of Dr Asa Breed. I was vaguely ill, still a little drunk from the night before. Dr Breed was driving. Tracks of a long-abandoned trolley system kept catching the wheels of his car.

Breed was a pink old man, very prosperous, beautifully dressed. His manner was civilized, optimistic, capable, serene. I, by contrast, felt bristly, diseased, cynical. I had spent the night with Sandra.

My soul seemed as foul as smoke from burning cat fur.

I thought the worst of everyone, and I knew some pretty sordid things about Dr Asa Breed, things Sandra had told me.

Sandra told me everyone in Ilium was sure that Dr Breed had been in love with Felix Hoenikker's wife. She told me that most people thought Breed was the father of all three Hoenikker children.

'Do you know Ilium at all?' Dr Breed suddenly asked me.

'This is my first visit.'

'It's a family town.'

'Sir?'

'There isn't much in the way of night life. Everybody's life pretty much centres around his family and his home.'

'That sounds very wholesome.'

'It is. We have very little juvenile delinquency.'

'Good.'

'Ilium has a very interesting history, you know.'

'That's very interesting.'

'It used to be the jumping-off place, you know.'

'Sir?'

'For the Western migration.'

'Oh.'

'People used to get outfitted here.'

'That's very interesting.'

'Just about where the Research Laboratory is now was the old stockade. That was where they held the public hangings, too, for the whole county.'

'I don't suppose crime paid any better then than it does now.'

'There was one man they hanged here in 1782 who had murdered twenty-six people. I've often thought somebody ought to do a book about him sometime. George Minor Moakely. He sang a song on the scaffold. He sang a song he'd composed for the occasion.'

'What was the song about?'

'You can find the words over at the Historical Society, if you're really interested.'

'I just wondered about the general tone.'

'He wasn't sorry about anything.'

'Some people are like that.'

'Think of it!' said Breed. 'Twenty-six people he had on his conscience!'

'The mind reels,' I said.

## 14 *When Automobiles Had Cut-glass Vases*

My sick head wobbled on my stiff neck. The trolley tracks had caught the wheels of Dr Breed's glossy Lincoln again.

I asked Dr Breed how many people were trying to reach the General Forge and Foundry Company by eight o'clock, and he told me thirty thousand.

Policemen in yellow raincapes were at every intersection, contradicting with their white-gloved hands what the stop-and-go signs said.

The stop-and-go signs, garish ghosts in the sleet, went through their irrelevant tomfoolery again and again, telling the glacier of automobiles what to do. Green meant go. Red meant stop. Orange meant change and caution.

Dr Breed told me that Dr Hoenikker, as a very young man, had simply abandoned his car in Ilium traffic one morning.

'The police, trying to find out what was holding up traffic,' he said, 'found Felix's car in the middle of everything, its motor running, a cigar burning in the ash tray, fresh flowers in the vases . . .'

'Vases?'

'It was a Marmon, about the size of a switch engine. It had little cut-glass vases on the doorposts, and Felix's wife used to put fresh flowers in the vases every morning. And there that car was in the middle of traffic.'

'Like the *Marie Celeste*,' I suggested.

'The Police Department hauled it away. They knew whose car it was, and they called up Felix, and they told him very politely where his car could be picked up. Felix told them they could keep it, that he didn't want it any more.'

'Did they?'

'No. They called up his wife, and she came and got the Marmon.'

'What was her name, by the way?'

'Emily.' Dr Breed licked his lips, and he got a faraway look, and he said the name of the woman, of the woman so long dead, again. 'Emily.'

'Do you think anybody would object if I used the story about the Marmon in my book?' I asked.

'As long as you don't use the end of it.'

'The *end* of it?'

'Emily wasn't used to driving the Marmon. She got into a bad wreck on the way home. It did something to her pelvis . . .' The traffic wasn't moving just then. Dr Breed closed his eyes and tightened his hands on the steering wheel.

'And that was why she died when little Newt was born.'

## 15 *Merry Christmas*

The Research Laboratory of the General Forge and Foundry Company was near the main gate of the company's Ilium works, about a city block from the executive parking lot where Dr Breed put his car.

I asked Dr Breed how many people worked for the Research Laboratory. 'Seven hundred,' he said, 'but less than a hundred are actually doing research. The other six hundred are all housekeepers in one way or another, and I am the chiefest housekeeper of all.'

When we joined the mainstream of mankind in the company street, a woman behind us wished Dr Breed a merry Christmas. Dr Breed turned to peer benignly into the sea of pale pies, and identified the greeter as one Miss Francine Pefko. Miss Pefko was twenty, vacantly pretty, and healthy – a dull normal.

In honour of the dulcitude of Christmastime, Dr Breed invited Miss Pefko to join us. He introduced her as the secretary of Dr Nilsak Horvath. He then told me who Horvath was. 'The famous surface chemist,' he said, 'the one who's doing such wonderful things with films.'

'What's new in surface chemistry?' I asked Miss Pefko.

'God,' she said, 'don't ask me. I just type what he tells me to type.' And then she apologized for having said 'God.'

'Oh, I think you understand more than you let on,' said Dr Breed.

'Not me.' Miss Pefko wasn't used to chatting with someone as important as Dr Breed and she was embarrassed. Her gait was affected, becoming stiff and chickenlike. Her smile was glassy, and she was ransacking her mind for something to say, finding nothing in it but used Kleenex and costume jewellery.

'Well . . .,' rumbled Dr Breed expansively, 'how do you like us, now that you've been with us – how long? Almost a year?'

'You scientists *think* too much,' blurted Miss Pefko. She laughed idiotically. Dr Breed's friendliness had blown every fuse in her nervous system. She was no longer responsible. 'You *all* think too much.'

A winded, defeated-looking fat woman in filthy coveralls trudged beside us, hearing what Miss Pefko said. She turned to examine Dr Breed, looking at him with helpless reproach. She hated people who thought too much. At that moment, she struck me as an appropriate representative for almost all mankind.

The fat woman's expression implied that she would go crazy on the spot if anybody did any more thinking.

'I think you'll find,' said Dr Breed, 'that everybody does about the same amount of thinking. Scientists simply think about things in one way, and other people think about things in others.'

'Ech,' gurgled Miss Pefko emptily. 'I take dictation from Dr Horvath and it's just like a foreign language. I don't think I'd understand – even if I was to go to college. And here he's maybe talking about something that's going to turn everything upside-down and inside-out like the atom bomb.

'When I used to come home from school Mother used to ask me what happened that day, and I'd tell her,' said Miss Pefko. 'Now I come home from work and she asks me the same question, and all I can say is – ' Miss Pefko shook her head and let her crimson lips flap slackly – 'I dunno, I dunno, I dunno.'

'If there's something you don't understand,' urged Dr Breed, 'ask Dr Horvath to explain it. He's very good at explaining.' He turned to me. 'Dr Hoenikker used to say that any scientist who couldn't explain to an eight-year-old what he was doing was a charlatan.'

'Then I'm dumber than an eight-year-old,' Miss Pefko mourned. 'I don't even know what a charlatan is.'

## 16 *Back to Kindergarten*

We climbed the four granite steps before the Research Laboratory. The building itself was of unadorned brick and rose six storeys. We passed between two heavily armed guards at the entrance.

Miss Pefko showed the guard on the left the pink *confidential* badge at the tip of her left breast.

Dr Breed showed the guard on our right the black *top-secret* badge on his soft lapel. Ceremoniously, Dr Breed put his arm around me without actually touching me, indicating to the guards that I was under his august protection and control.

I smiled at one of the guards. He did not smile back. There was nothing funny about national security, nothing at all.

Dr Breed, Miss Pefko, and I moved thoughtfully through the Laboratory's grand foyer to the elevators.

'Ask Dr Horvath to explain something sometime,' said Dr Breed to Miss Pefko. 'See if you don't get a nice, clear answer.'

'He'd have to start back in the first grade – or maybe even kindergarten,' she said. 'I missed a lot.'

'We *all* missed a lot,' Dr Breed agreed. 'We'd *all* do well to start over again, preferably with kindergarten.'

We watched the Laboratory's receptionist turn on the many educational exhibits that lined the foyer's walls. The receptionist was a tall, thin girl – icy, pale. At her crisp touch, lights twinkled, wheels turned, flasks bubbled, bells rang.

'Magic,' declared Miss Pefko.

'I'm sorry to hear a member of the Laboratory family using that brackish, medieval word,' said Dr Breed. 'Every one of those exhibits explains itself. They're designed so as *not* to be mystifying. They're the very antithesis of magic.'

'The very what of magic?'

'The exact opposite of magic.'

'You couldn't prove it by me.'

Dr Breed looked just a little peeved. 'Well,' he said, 'we don't *want* to mystify. At least give us credit for that.'

## 17 The Girl Pool

Dr Breed's secretary was standing on her desk in his outer office tying an accordion-pleated Christmas bell to the ceiling fixture.

'Look here, Naomi,' cried Dr Breed, 'we've gone six months without a fatal accident! Don't you spoil it by falling off the desk!'

Miss Naomi Faust was a merry, desiccated old lady. I suppose she had served Dr Breed for almost all his life, and her life, too. She laughed. 'I'm indestructible. And, even if I did fall, Christmas angels would catch me.'

'They've been known to miss.'

Two paper tendrils, also accordion-pleated, hung down from the clapper of the bell. Miss Faust pulled one. It unfolded stickily and became a long banner with a message written on it. 'Here,' said Miss Faust, handing the free end to Dr Breed, 'pull it the rest of the way and tack the end to the bulletin board.'

Dr Breed obeyed, stepping back to read the banner's message. 'Peace on Earth!' he read out loud heartily.

Miss Faust stepped down from her desk with the other tendril, unfolding it. 'Good Will Toward Men!' the other tendril said.

'By golly,' chuckled Dr Breed, 'they've dehydrated Christmas! The place looks festive, very festive.'

'And I remembered the chocolate bars for the Girl Pool, too,' she said. 'Aren't you proud of me?'

Dr Breed touched his forehead, dismayed by his forgetfulness. 'Thank God for that! It slipped my mind.'

'We mustn't ever forget that,' said Miss Faust. 'It's a tradition now – Dr Breed and his chocolate bars for the Girl Pool at Christmas.' She explained to me that the Girl Pool was the typing bureau in the Laboratory's basement. 'The girls belong to anybody with access to a dictaphone.'

All year long, she said, the girls of the Girl Pool listened to the faceless voices of scientists on dictaphone records – records brought in by mail girls. Once a year the girls left their cloister of cement block to go a-carolling – to get their chocolate bars from Dr Asa Breed.

'They serve science, too,' Dr Breed testified, 'even though they may not understand a word of it. God bless them, every one!'

## 18 The Most Valuable Commodity on Earth

When we got into Dr Breed's inner office, I attempted to put my thoughts in order for a sensible interview. I found that my mental health had not improved. And, when I started to ask Dr Breed questions about the day of the bomb, I found that the public-relations centres of my brain had been suffocated by booze and burning cat fur. Every question I asked implied that the creators of the atomic bomb had been criminal accessories to murder most foul.

Dr Breed was astonished, and then he got very sore. He drew back from me and he grumbled, 'I gather you don't like scientists very much.'

'I wouldn't say that, sir.'

'All your questions seem aimed at getting me to admit that scientists are heartless, conscienceless, narrow boobies, indifferent to the fate of the rest of the human race, or maybe not really members of the human race at all.'

'That's putting it pretty strong.'

'No stronger than what you're going to put in your book, apparently. I thought that what you were after was a fair, objective biography of Felix Hoenikker – certainly as significant a task as a young writer could assign himself in this day and age. But no, you come here with preconceived notions about mad scientists. Where did you ever get such ideas? From the funny papers?'

'From Dr Hoenikker's son, to name one source.'

'Which son?'

'Newton,' I said. I had little Newt's letter with me, and I showed it to him. 'How small is Newt, by the way?'

'No bigger than an umbrella stand,' said Dr Breed, reading Newt's letter and frowning.

'The other two children are normal?'

'Of course! I hate to disappoint you, but scientists have children just like anybody else's children.'

I did my best to calm down Dr Breed, to convince him that I was really interested in an accurate portrait of Dr Hoenikker. 'I've come here with no purpose than to set down exactly what you tell me about Dr Hoenikker. Newt's letter was just a beginning, and I'll balance off against it whatever you can tell me.'

'I'm sick of people misunderstanding what a scientist is, what a scientist does.'

'I'll do my best to clear up the misunderstanding.'

'In this country most people don't even understand what pure research is.'

'I'd appreciate it if you'd tell me what it is.'

'It isn't looking for a better cigarette filter or a softer face tissue or a longer-lasting house paint, God help us. Everybody talks about research and practically nobody in this country's doing it. We're one of the few companies that actually hires men to do pure research. When most other companies brag about their research, they're talking about industrial hack technicians who wear white coats, work out of cookbooks, and dream up an improved windshield wiper for next year's Oldsmobile.'

'But here . . . ?'

'Here, and shockingly few other places in this country, men are paid to increase knowledge, to work towards no end but that.'

'That's very generous of General Forge and Foundry Company.'

'Nothing generous about it. New knowledge is the most valuable commodity on earth. The more truth we have to work with, the richer we become.'

Had I been a Bokononist then, that statement would have made me howl.

## 19 No More Mud

'Do you mean,' I said to Dr Breed, 'that nobody in this Laboratory is ever told what to work on? Nobody even *suggests* what they work on?'

'People suggest things all the time, but it isn't in the nature of a pure-research man to pay any attention to suggestions. His head is full of projects of his own, and that's the way we want it.'

'Did anybody ever try to suggest projects to Dr Hoenikker?'

'Certainly. Admirals and generals in particular. They looked upon him as a sort of magician who could make America invincible with a wave of his wand. They brought all kinds of crackpot schemes up here – still do. The only thing wrong with the schemes is that, given our present state of knowledge, the schemes won't work. Scientists of the order of Dr Hoenikker are supposed to fill the little gaps. I remember, shortly before Felix died, there was a Marine general who was hounding him to do something about mud.'

'Mud?'

'The Marines, after almost two hundred years of wallowing in mud, were sick of it,' said Dr Breed. 'The general, as their spokesman, felt that one of the aspects of progress should be that Marines no longer had to fight in mud.'

'What did the general have in mind?'

'The absence of mud. No more mud.'

'I suppose,' I theorized, 'it might be possible with mountains of some sort of chemical, or tons of some sort of machinery . . .'

'What the general had in mind was a little pill or a little machine. Not only were the Marines sick of mud, they were sick of carrying cumbersome objects. They wanted something *little* to carry for a change.'

'What did Dr Hoenikker say?'

'In his playful way, and *all* his ways were playful, Felix suggested that there might be a single grain of something – even a microscopic grain – that could make infinite expanses of muck, marsh, swamp, creeks, pools, quicksand, and mire as solid as this desk.'

Dr Breed banged his speckled old fist on the desk. The desk was a kidney-shaped, sea green steel affair. 'One Marine could carry more than enough of the stuff to free an armoured division bogged down in the Everglades. According to Felix, one Marine could carry enough of the stuff to do that under the nail of his little finger.'

'That's impossible.'

'You would say so, I would say so – practically everybody would say so. To Felix, in his playful way, it was entirely possible. The miracle of Felix – and I sincerely hope you'll put this in your book somewhere – was that he always approached old puzzles as though they were brand new.'

'I feel like Francine Pefko now,' I said, 'and all the girls in the Girl Pool, too. Dr Hoenikker could never have explained to me how something that could be carried under a fingernail could make a swamp as solid as your desk.'

'I told you what a good explainer Felix was . . .'

'Even so . . .'

'He was able to explain it to me,' said Dr Breed, 'and I'm sure I can explain it to you. The puzzle is how to get Marines out of the mud – right?'

'Right.'

'All right,' said Dr Breed, 'listen carefully. Here we go.'

## 20 *Ice-nine*

'There are several ways,' Dr Breed said to me, 'in which certain liquids can crystallize – can freeze – several ways in which their atoms can stack and lock in an orderly, rigid way.'

That old man with spotted hands invited me to think of the several ways in which cannon balls might be stacked on a court-house lawn, of the several ways in which oranges might be packed into a crate.

'So it is with atoms in crystals, too; and two different crystals of the same substance can have quite different physical properties.'

He told me about a factory that had been growing big crystals of ethylene diamine tartrate. The crystals were useful in certain manufacturing operations, he said. But one day the factory discovered that the crystals it was growing no longer had the properties desired. The atoms had begun to stack and lock – to freeze – in a different fashion. The liquid that was crystallizing hadn't changed, but the crystals it was forming were, as far as industrial applications went, pure junk.

How this had come about was a mystery. The theoretical villain, however, was what Dr Breed called 'a seed'. He meant by that a tiny grain of the undesired crystal pattern. The seed, which had come from God-only-knows-where, taught the atoms the novel way in which to stack and lock, to crystallize, to freeze.

'Now think about cannon balls on a court-house lawn or about oranges in a crate again,' he suggested. And he helped me to see that the pattern of the bottom layer of cannon balls or of oranges determined how each subsequent layer would stack and lock. 'The bottom layer is the seed of how every cannon ball or every orange that comes after is going to behave, even to an infinite number of cannon balls or oranges.

'Now suppose,' chortled Dr Breed, enjoying himself, 'that there were many possible ways in which water could crystallize, could freeze. Suppose that the sort of ice we skate upon and put into highballs – what we might call *ice-one* – is only one of several types of ice. Suppose water always froze as *ice-one* on Earth because it had never had a seed to teach it how to form *ice-two, ice-three, ice-four . . .*? And suppose,' he rapped on his desk with his old hand again, 'that there were one form, which we will call *ice-nine* – a crystal as hard as this desk – with a melting point of, let us say, one hundred degrees Fahrenheit, or, better still, a melting point of one hundred and thirty degrees.'

'All right, I'm still with you,' I said.

Dr Breed was interrupted by whispers in his outer office, whispers loud and portentous. They were the sounds of the Girl Pool.

The girls were preparing to sing in the outer office.

And they did sing, as Dr Breed and I appeared in the doorway. Each of about a hundred girls had made herself into a choirgirl by putting on a collar of white bond paper, secured by a paper clip. They sang beautifully.

I was surprised and mawkishly heartbroken. I am always moved by that seldom-used treasure, the sweetness with which most girls can sing.

The girls sang 'O Little Town of Bethlehem'. I am not likely to forget very soon their interpretation of the line:

'The hopes and fears of all the years are here with us tonight.'

## 21 *The Marines March On*

When old Dr Breed, with the help of Miss Faust, had passed out the Christmas chocolate bars to the girls, we returned to his office.

There, he said to me, 'Where were we? Oh yes!' And that old man asked me to think of United States Marines in a Godforsaken swamp.

'Their trucks and tanks and howitzers are wallowing,' he complained, 'sinking in stinking miasma and ooze.'

He raised a finger and winked at me. 'But suppose, young man, that one Marine had with him a tiny capsule containing a seed of *ice-nine*, a new way for the atoms of water to stack and lock, to freeze. If that Marine threw that seed into the nearest puddle . . . ?'

'The puddle would freeze?' I guessed.

'And all the muck around the puddle?'

'It would freeze?'

'And all the puddles in the frozen muck?'

'They would freeze?'

'And the pools and the streams in the frozen muck?'

'They would freeze?'

'You *bet* they would!' he cried. 'And the United States Marines would rise from the swamp and march on!'

## 22 *Member of the Yellow Press*

'There *is* such stuff?' I asked.

'No, no, no, no,' said Dr Breed, losing patience with me again. 'I only told you all this in order to give you some insight into the extraordinary novelty of the ways in which Felix was likely to approach an old problem. What I've just told you is what he told the Marine general who was hounding him about mud.

'Felix ate alone here in the cafeteria every day. It was a rule that no one was to sit with him, to interrupt his chain of thought. But the Marine general barged in, pulled up a chair, and started talking about mud. What I've told you was Felix's offhand reply.'

'There – there really *isn't* such a thing?'

'I just told you there wasn't!' cried Dr Breed hotly. 'Felix died shortly after that! And, if you'd been listening to what I've been trying to tell you about pure-research men, you wouldn't ask such a question! Pure-research men work on what fascinates them, not on what fascinates other people.'

'I keep thinking about that swamp . . .'

'You can *stop* thinking about it! I've made the only point I wanted to make with the swamp.'

'If the streams flowing through the swamp froze as *ice-nine*, what about the rivers and lakes the streams fed?'

'They'd freeze. But there is no such thing as *ice-nine*.'

'And the oceans the frozen rivers fed?'

'They'd freeze, of course,' he snapped. 'I suppose you're going to rush to market with a sensational story about *ice-nine* now. I tell you again, it does not exist!'

'And the springs feeding the frozen lakes and streams, and all the water underground feeding the springs?'

'They'd freeze, damn it!' he cried. 'But if I had known that you were a member of the yellow press,' he said grandly, rising to his feet, 'I wouldn't have wasted a minute with you!'

'And the rain?'

'When it fell, it would freeze into hard hobnails of *ice-nine* – and that would be the end of the world! And the end of the interview, too! Good-bye!'

## 23 *The Last Batch of Brownies*

Dr Breed was mistaken about at least one thing: there was such a thing as *ice-nine*.

And *ice-nine* was on earth.

*Ice-nine* was the last gift Felix Hoenikker created for mankind before going to his just reward.

He did it without anyone's realizing what he was doing. He did it without leaving records of what he'd done.

True, elaborate apparatus was necessary in the act of creation, but it already existed in the Research Laboratory. Dr Hoenikker had only to go calling on Laboratory neighbours – borrowing this and that, making a winsome neighbourhood nuisance of himself – until, so to speak, he had baked his last batch of brownies.

He had made a chip of *ice-nine*. It was blue-white. It had a melting point of one hundred fourteen point four degrees Fahrenheit.

Felix Hoenikker had put the chip in a little bottle; and he put the bottle in his pocket. And he had gone to his cottage on Cape Cod with his three children, there intending to celebrate Christmas.

Angela had been thirty-four. Frank had been twenty-four. Little Newt had been eighteen.

The old man had died on Christmas Eve, having told only his children about *ice-nine*.

His children had divided the *ice-nine* among themselves.

## 24  *What a* Wampeter *Is*

Which brings me to the Bokononist concept of a *wampeter*.

A *wampeter* is the pivot of a *karass*. No *karass* is without a *wampeter*, Bokonon tells us, just as no wheel is without a hub.

Anything can be a *wampeter*: a tree, a rock, an animal, an idea, a book, a melody, the Holy Grail. Whatever it is, the members of its *karass* revolve about it in the majestic chaos of a spiral of nebula. The orbits of the members of a *karass* about their common *wampeter* are spiritual orbits, naturally. It is souls and not bodies that revolve. As Bokonon invites us to sing:

> Around and around and around we spin,
> With feet of lead and wings of tin . . .

And *wampeters* come and *wampeters* go, Bokonon tells us.

At any given time a *karass* actually has two *wampeters* – one waxing in importance, one waning.

And I am almost certain that while I was talking to Dr Breed in Ilium, the *wampeter* of my *karass* that was just coming into bloom was that crystalline form of water, that blue-white gem, that seed of doom called *ice-nine*.

While I was talking to Dr Breed in Ilium, Angela, Franklin, and Newton Hoenikker had in their possession seeds of *ice-nine*, seeds grown from their father's seed – chips, in a manner of speaking, off the old block.

What was to become of those three chips was, I am convinced, a principal concern of my *karass*.

## 25  The Main Thing About Dr Hoenikker

So much, for now, for the *wampeter* of my *karass*.

After my unpleasant interview with Dr Breed in the Research Laboratory of the General Forge and Foundry Company, I was put into the hands of Miss Faust. Her orders were to show me the door. I prevailed upon her, however, to show me the laboratory of the late Dr Hoenikker first.

En route, I asked her how well she had known Dr Hoenikker. She gave me a frank and interesting reply, and a piquant smile to go with it.

'I don't think he was knowable. I mean, when most people talk about knowing somebody a lot or a little, they're talking about secrets they've been told or haven't been told. They're talking about intimate things, family things, love things,' that nice old lady said to me. 'Dr Hoenikker had all those things in his life, the way every living person has to, but they weren't the main things with him.'

'What *were* the main things?' I asked her.

'Dr Breed keeps telling me the main thing with Dr Hoenikker was truth.'

'You don't seem to agree.'

'I don't know whether I agree or not. I just have trouble understanding how truth, all by itself, could be enough for a person.'

Miss Faust was ripe for Bokononism.

## 26 What God Is

'Did you ever talk to Dr Hoenikker?' I asked Miss Faust.

'Oh, certainly. I talked to him a lot.'

'Do any conversations stick in your mind?'

'There was one where he bet I couldn't tell him anything that was absolutely true. So I said to him, "God is love."'

'And what did he say?'

'He said, "What is God? What is love?"'

'Um.'

'But God really *is* love, you know,' said Miss Faust, 'no matter what Dr Hoenikker said.'

## 27 Men from Mars

The room that had been the laboratory of Dr Felix Hoenikker was on the sixth floor, the top floor of the building.

A purple cord had been stretched across the doorway, and a brass plate on the wall explained why the room was sacred:

IN THIS ROOM, DR FELIX HOENIKKER, NOBEL LAUREATE IN PHYSICS, SPENT THE LAST TWENTY-EIGHT YEARS OF HIS LIFE. 'WHERE HE WAS, THERE WAS THE FRONTIER OF KNOWLEDGE.' THE IMPORTANCE OF THIS ONE MAN IN THE HISTORY OF MANKIND IS INCALCULABLE

Miss Faust offered to unshackle the purple cord for me so that I might go inside and traffic more intimately with whatever ghosts there were.

I accepted.

'It's just as he left it,' she said, 'except that there were rubber bands all over one counter.'

'Rubber bands?'

'Don't ask me what for. Don't ask me what any of all this is for.'

The old man had left the laboratory a mess. What engaged my attention at once was the quantity of cheap toys lying around. There was a paper kite with a broken spine. There was a toy gyroscope, wound with string, ready to whirr and balance itself. There was a top. There was a bubble pipe. There was a fish bowl with a castle and two turtles in it.

'He loved ten-cent stores,' said Miss Faust.

'I can see he did.'

'Some of his most famous experiments were performed with equipment that cost less than a dollar.'

'A penny saved is a penny earned.'

There were numerous pieces of conventional laboratory equipment, too, of course, but they seemed drab accessories to the cheap, gay toys.

Dr Hoenikker's desk was piled with correspondence.

'I don't think he ever answered a letter,' mused Miss Faust. 'People had to get him on the telephone or come to see him if they wanted an answer.'

There was a framed photograph on his desk. Its back was towards me and I ventured a guess as to whose picture it was. 'His wife?'

'No.'

'One of his children?'

'No.'

'Himself?'

'No.'

So I took a look. I found that the picture was of an humble little war memorial in front of a small-town court-house. Part of the memorial was a sign that gave the names of those villagers who had died in various wars, and I thought that the sign must be the reason for the photograph. I could read the names, and I half expected to find the name Hoenikker among them. It wasn't there.

'That was one of his hobbies,' said Miss Faust.

'What was?'

'Photographing how cannon balls are stacked on different court-house lawns. Apparently how they've got them stacked in that picture is very unusual.'

'I see.'

'He was an unusual man.'

'I agree.'

'Maybe in a million years everybody will be as smart as he was and see things the way he did. But, compared with the average person of today, he was as different as a man from Mars.'

'Maybe he really *was* a Martian,' I suggested.

'That would certainly go a long way towards explaining his three strange kids.'

## 28 Mayonnaise

While Miss Faust and I waited for an elevator to take us to the first floor, Miss Faust said she hoped the elevator that came would not be number five. Before I could ask her why this was a reasonable wish, number five arrived.

Its operator was a small and ancient Negro whose name was Lyman Enders Knowles. Knowles was insane, I'm almost sure – offensively so, in that he grabbed his own behind and cried, 'Yes, yes!' whenever he felt that he'd made a point.

'Hello, fellow anthropoids and lily pads and paddlewheels,' he said to Miss Faust and me. 'Yes, yes!'

'First floor, please,' said Miss Faust coldly.

All Knowles had to do to close the door and get us to the first floor was to press a button, but he wasn't going to do that yet. He wasn't going to do it, maybe, for years.

'Man told me,' he said, 'that these here elevators was Mayan architecture. I never knew that till today. And I says to him, "What's that make me – mayonnaise?" Yes, yes! And while he was thinking that over, I hit him with a question that straightened him up and made him think twice as hard! Yes, yes!'

'Could we please go down, Mr Knowles?' begged Miss Faust.

'I said to him,' said Knowles, '"This here's a *re*-search laboratory. *Re*-search means *look again*, don't it? Means they're looking for something they found once and it got away somehow, and now they got to *re*-search for it! How come they got to build a building like this, with mayonnaise elevators and all, and fill it with all these crazy people? What is it they're trying to find again? Who lost what?" Yes, yes!'

'That's very interesting,' sighed Miss Faust. 'Now, could we go down?'

'Only way we *can* go is down,' barked Knowles. 'This here's the top. You ask me to go up and wouldn't be a thing I could do for you. Yes, yes!'

'So let's go down,' said Miss Faust.

'Very soon now. This gentleman here been paying his respects to Dr Hoenikker?'

'Yes,' I said. 'Did you know him?'

'*Intimately*,' he said. 'You know what I said when he died?'

'No.'

'I said, "Dr Hoenikker – he ain't dead."'

'Oh?'

'Just entered a new dimension. Yes, yes!'

He punched a button, and down we went.

'Did you know the Hoenikker children?' I asked him.

'Babies full of rabies,' he said. 'Yes, yes!'

## 29 *Gone, but Not Forgotten*

There was one more thing I wanted to do in Ilium. I wanted to get a photograph of the old man's tomb. So I went back to my room, found Sandra gone, picked up my camera, hired a cab.

Sleet was still coming down, acid and grey. I thought the old man's tombstone in all that sleet might photograph pretty well, might even make a good picture for the jacket of *The Day the World Ended*.

The custodian at the cemetery gate told me how to find the Hoenikker burial plot. 'Can't miss it,' he said. 'It's got the biggest marker in the place.'

He did not lie. The marker was an alabaster phallus twenty feet high and three feet thick. It was plastered with sleet.

'By God,' I exclaimed, getting out of the cab with my camera, 'how's that for a suitable memorial to a father of the atom bomb?' I laughed.

I asked the driver if he'd mind standing by the monument in order to give some idea of scale. And then I asked him to wipe away some of the sleet so the name of the deceased would show.

He did so.

And there on the shaft in letters six inches high, so help me God, was the word:

MOTHER

## 30  *Only Sleeping*

'Mother?' asked the driver, incredulously.

I wiped away more sleet and uncovered this poem:

> Mother, Mother, how I pray
> For you to guard us every day.
> – ANGELA HOENIKKER

And under this poem was yet another:

> You are not dead,
> But only sleeping.
> We should smile,
> And stop our weeping.
> – FRANKLIN HOENIKKER

And underneath this, inset in the shaft, was a square of cement bearing the imprint of an infant's hand. Beneath the imprint were the words:

BABY NEWT

'If that's Mother,' said the driver, 'what in hell could they have raised over Father?' He made an obscene suggestion as to what the appropriate marker might be.

We found Father close by. His memorial – as specified in his will, I later discovered – was a marble cube forty centimetres on each side.

'FATHER', it said.

## 31 *Another Breed*

As we were leaving the cemetery the driver of the cab worried about the condition of his own mother's grave. He asked if I would mind taking a short detour to look at it.

It was a pathetic little stone that marked his mother – not that it mattered.

And the driver asked me if I would mind another brief detour, this time to a tombstone salesroom across the street from the cemetery.

I wasn't a Bokononist then, so I agreed with some peevishness. As a Bokononist, of course, I would have agreed gaily to go anywhere anyone suggested. As Bokonon says: 'Peculiar travel suggestions are dancing lessons from God.'

The name of the tombstone establishment was Avram Breed and Sons. As the driver talked to the salesman I wandered among the monuments – blank monuments, monuments in memory of nothing so far.

I found a little institutional joke in the showroom: over a stone angel hung mistletoe. Cedar boughs were heaped on her pedestal, and around her marble throat was a necklace of Christmas tree lamps.

'How much for her?' I asked the salesman.

'Not for sale. She's a hundred years old. My great-grandfather, Avram Breed, carved her.'

'This business is that old?'

'That's right.'

'And you're a Breed?'

'The fourth generation in this location.'

'Any relation to Dr Asa Breed, the director of the Research Laboratory?'

'His brother.' He said his name was Marvin Breed.

'It's a small world,' I observed.

'When you put it in a cemetery, it is.' Marvin Breed was a sleek and vulgar, a smart and sentimental man.

## 32  Dynamite Money

'I just came from your brother's office. I'm a writer. I was interviewing him about Dr Hoenikker,' I said to Marvin Breed.

'There was one queer son of a bitch. Not my brother; I mean Hoenikker.'

'Did you sell him that monument for his wife?'

'I sold his kids that. He never got around to putting any kind of marker on her grave. And then, after she'd been dead for a year or more, Hoenikker's three kids came in here – the big tall girl, the boy, and the little baby. They wanted the biggest stone money could buy, and the two older ones had poems they'd written. They wanted the poems on the stone.

'You can laugh at that stone, if you want to,' said Marvin Breed, 'but those kids got more consolation out of that than anything else money could have bought. They used to come and look at it and put flowers on it I-don't-know-how-many-times a year.'

'It must have cost a lot.'

'Nobel Prize money bought it. Two things that money bought: a cottage on Cape Cod and that monument.'

'Dynamite money,' I marvelled, thinking of the violence of dynamite and the absolute repose of a tombstone and a summer home.

'What?'

'Nobel invented dynamite.'

'Well, I guess it takes all kinds . . .'

Had I been a Bokononist then, pondering the miraculously intricate chain of events that had brought dynamite money to that particular tombstone company, I might have whispered, 'Busy, busy, busy.'

*Busy, busy, busy*, is what we Bokononists whisper whenever we think of how complicated and unpredictable the machinery of life really is.

But all I could say as a Christian then was, 'Life is sure funny sometimes.'

'And sometimes it isn't,' said Marvin Breed.


## 33 *An Ungrateful Man*

I asked Marvin Breed if he'd known Emily Hoenikker, the wife of Felix; the mother of Angela, Frank, and Newt; the woman under that monstrous shaft.

'Know her?' His voice turned tragic. 'Did I *know* her, mister? Sure, I knew her. I knew Emily. We went to Ilium High together. We were co-chairmen of the Class Colours Committee then. Her father owned the Ilium Music Store. She could play every musical instrument there was. I fell so hard for her I gave up football and tried to play the violin. And then my big brother Asa came home for spring vacation from M.I.T., and I made the mistake of introducing him to my best girl.' Marvin Breed snapped his fingers. 'He took her away from me just like that. I smashed up my seventy-five-dollar violin on a big brass knob at the foot of my bed, and I went down to a florist shop and got the kind of box they put a dozen roses in, and I put the busted fiddle in the box, and I sent it to her by Western Union messenger boy.'

'Pretty, was she?'

'Pretty?' he echoed. 'Mister, when I see my first lady angel, if God ever sees fit to show me one, it'll be her wings and not her face that'll make my mouth fall open. I've already seen the prettiest face that ever could be. There wasn't a man in Ilium County who wasn't in love with her, secretly or otherwise. She could have had any man she wanted.' He spat on his own floor. 'And she had to go and marry that little Dutch son of a bitch! She was engaged to my brother, and then that sneaky little bastard hit town.' Marvin Breed snapped his fingers again. 'He took her away from my big brother like that.

'I suppose it's high treason and ungrateful and ignorant and backward and anti-intellectual to call a dead man as famous as Felix Hoenikker a son of a bitch. I know all about how harmless and gentle and dreamy he was supposed to be, how he'd never hurt a fly, how he didn't care about money and power and fancy clothes and automobiles and things, how he wasn't like the rest of us, how he was better than the rest of us, how he was so innocent he was practically a Jesus – except for the Son of God part . . .'

Marvin Breed felt it was unnecessary to complete his thought. I had to ask him to do it.

'But what?' he said. 'But what?' He went to a window looking out at the cemetery gate. 'But what,' he murmured at the gate and the sleet and the Hoenikker shaft that could be dimly seen.

'But,' he said, 'but how the hell innocent is a man who helps make a thing like an atomic bomb? And how can you say a man had a good mind when he couldn't even bother to do anything when the best-hearted, most beautiful woman in the world, his own wife, was dying for lack of love and understanding . . .'

He shuddered, 'Sometimes I wonder if he wasn't born dead. I never met a man who was less interested in the living. Sometimes I think that's the trouble with the world: too many people in high places who are stone-cold dead.'

## 34 Vin-dit

It was in the tombstone salesroom that I had my first *vin-dit*, a Bokononist word meaning a sudden, very personal shove in the direction of Bokononism, in the direction of believing that God Almighty knew all about me after all, that God Almighty had some pretty elaborate plans for me.

The *vin-dit* had to do with the stone angel under the mistletoe. The cab driver had gotten it into his head that he had to have that angel for his mother's grave at any price. He was standing in front of it with tears in his eyes.

Marvin Breed was still staring out the window at the cemetery gate, having just said his piece about Felix Hoenikker. 'The little Dutch son of a bitch may have been a modern holy man,' he added, 'but Goddamn if he ever did anything he didn't want to, and Goddamn if he didn't get everything he ever wanted.

'Music,' he said.

'Pardon me?' I asked.

'That's why she married him. She said his mind was tuned to the biggest music there was, the music of the stars.' He shook his head. 'Crap.'

And then the gate reminded him of the last time he'd seen Frank Hoenikker, the model-maker, the tormentor of bugs in jars. 'Frank,' he said.

'What about him?'

'The last I saw of that poor, queer kid was when he came out through that cemetery gate. His father's funeral was still going on. The old man wasn't underground yet, and out through that gate came Frank. He raised his thumb at the first car that came by. It was a new Pontiac with a Florida licence plate. It stopped. Frank got in it, and that was the last anybody in Ilium ever saw of him.'

'I hear he's wanted by the police.'

'That was an accident, a freak. Frank wasn't any criminal. He didn't have that kind of nerve. The only work he was any good at was model-making. The only job he ever held onto was at Jack's Hobby Shop, selling models, making models, giving people advice on how to make models. When he cleared out of here, went to Florida, he got a job in a model shop in Sarasota. Turned out the model shop was a front for a ring that stole Cadillacs, ran 'em straight on board old L.S.T.s and shipped 'em to Cuba. That's how Frank got balled up in all that. I expect the reason the cops haven't found him is he's dead. He just heard too much while he was sticking turrets on the battleship *Missouri* with Duco Cement.'

'Where's Newt now, do you know?'

'Guess he's with his sister in Indianapolis. Last I heard was he got mixed up with that Russian midget and flunked out of pre-med at Cornell. Can you imagine a midget trying to become a doctor? And, in that same miserable family, there's that great big, gawky girl, over six feet tall. That man, who's so famous for having a great mind, he pulled that girl out of high school in her sophomore year so he could go on having some woman take care of him. All she had going for her was the clarinet she'd played in the Ilium High School band, the Marching Hundred.

'After she left school,' said Breed, 'nobody ever asked her out. She didn't have any friends, and the old man never even thought to give her any money to go anywhere. You know what she used to do?'

'Nope.'

'Every so often at night she'd lock herself in her room and she'd play records, and she'd play along with the records on her clarinet. The miracle of this age, as far as I'm concerned, is that that woman ever got herself a husband.'

'How much do you want for this angel?' asked the cab driver.

'I've told you, it's not for sale.'

'I don't suppose there's anybody around who can do that kind of stone cutting any more,' I observed.

'I've got a nephew who can,' said Breed. 'Asa's boy. He was all set to be a heap-big *re*-search scientist, and then they dropped the bomb on Hiroshima and the kid quit, and he got drunk, and he came out here, and he told me he wanted to go to work cutting stone.'

'He works here now?'

'He's a sculptor in Rome.'

'If somebody offered you enough,' said the driver, 'you'd take it, wouldn't you?'

'Might. But it would take a lot of money.'

'Where would you put the name on a thing like that?' asked the driver.

'There's already a name on it – on the pedestal.' We couldn't see the name, because of the boughs banked against the pedestal.

'It was never called for?' I wanted to know.

'It was never *paid* for. The way the story goes: this German immigrant was on his way West with his wife, and she died of smallpox here in Ilium. So he ordered this angel to be put up over her, and he showed my great-grandfather he had the cash to pay for it. But then he was robbed. Somebody took practically every cent he had. All he had left in this world was some land he'd bought in Indiana, land he'd never seen. So he moved on – said he'd be back later to pay for the angel.'

'But he never came back?' I asked.

'Nope.' Marvin Breed nudged some of the boughs aside with his toe so that we could see the raised letters on the pedestal. There was a last name written there. 'There's a screwy name for you,' he said. 'If that immigrant had any descendants, I expect they Americanized the name. They're probably Jones or Black or Thompson now.'

'There you're wrong,' I murmured.

The room seemed to tip, and its walls and ceiling and floor were transformed momentarily into the mouths of many tunnels – tunnels leading in all directions through time. I had a Bokononist vision of the unity in every second of all time and all wandering mankind, all wandering womankind, all wandering children.

'There you're wrong,' I said, when the vision was gone.

'You know some people by that name?'

'Yes.'

The name was my last name, too.

## 35 *Hobby Shop*

On the way back to the hotel I caught sight of Jack's Hobby Shop, the place where Franklin Hoenikker had worked. I told the cab driver to stop and wait.

I went in and found Jack himself presiding over his teeny-weeny fire engines, railroad trains, airplanes, boats, houses, lamp posts, trees, tanks, rockets, automobiles, porters, conductors, policemen, firemen, mommies, daddies, cats, dogs, chickens, soldiers, ducks, and cows. He was a cadaverous man, a serious man, a dirty man, and he coughed a lot.

'What kind of a boy was Franklin Hoenikker?' he echoed, and he coughed and coughed. He shook his head, and he showed me that he adored Frank as much as he'd ever adored anybody. 'That isn't a question I have to answer with words. I can *show* you what kind of a boy Franklin Hoenikker was.' He coughed. 'You can look,' he said, 'and you can judge for yourself.'

And he took me down into the basement of his store. He lived down there. There was a double bed and a dresser and a hot plate.

Jack apologized for the unmade bed. 'My wife left me a week ago.' He coughed. 'I'm still trying to pull the strings of my life back together.'

And then he turned on a switch, and the far end of the basement was filled with a blinding light.

We approached the light and found that it was sunshine to a fantastic little country built on plywood, an island as perfectly rectangular as a township in Kansas. Any restless soul, any soul seeking to find what lay beyond its green boundaries, really would fall off the edge of the world.

The details were so exquisitely in scale, so cunningly textured and tinted, that it was unnecessary for me to squint in order to believe that the nation was real – the hills, the lakes, the rivers, the forests, the towns, and all else that good natives everywhere hold so dear.

And everywhere ran a spaghetti pattern of railroad tracks.

'Look at the doors of the houses,' said Jack reverently.

'Neat. Keen.'

'They've got real knobs on 'em, and the knockers really work.'

'God.'

'You ask what kind of a boy Franklin Hoenikker was; he built this.' Jack choked up.

'All by himself?'

'Oh, I helped some, but anything I did was according to his plans. That kid was a genius.'

'How could anybody argue with you?'

'His kid brother was a midget, you know.'

'I know.'

'He did some of the soldering underneath.'

'It sure looks real.'

'It wasn't easy, and it wasn't done overnight, either.'

'Rome wasn't built in a day.'

'That kid didn't have any home life, you know.'

'I've heard.'

'This was his real home. Thousands of hours he spent down here. Sometimes he wouldn't even run the trains; just sit and look, the way we're doing.'

'There's a lot to see. It's practically like a trip to Europe, there are so many things to see, if you look close.'

'He'd see things you and I wouldn't see. He'd all of a sudden tear down a hill that would look just as real as any hill you ever saw – to you and me. And he'd be right, too. He'd put a lake where that hill had been and a trestle over the lake, and it would look ten times as good as it did before.'

'It isn't a talent everybody has.'

'That's right!' said Jack passionately. The passion cost him another coughing fit. When the fit was over, his eyes were watering copiously. 'Listen, I told that kid he should go to college and study some engineering so he could go to work for American Flyer or somebody like that – somebody big, somebody who'd really back all the ideas he had.'

'Looks to me as if you backed him a good deal.'

'Wish I had, wish I could have,' mourned Jack. 'I didn't have the capital. I gave him stuff whenever I could, but most of this stuff he bought out of what he earned working upstairs for me. He didn't spend a dime on anything but this – didn't drink, didn't smoke, didn't go to movies, didn't go out with girls, wasn't car crazy.'

'This country could certainly use a few more of those.'

Jack shrugged. 'Well . . . I guess the Florida gangsters got him. Afraid he'd talk.'

'Guess they did.'

Jack suddenly broke down and cried. 'I wonder if those dirty sons of bitches,' he sobbed, 'have any idea what it was they killed!'

## 36 Miaow

During my trip to Ilium and to points beyond – a two-week expedition bridging Christmas – I let a poor poet named Sherman Krebbs have my New York City apartment free. My second wife had left me on the grounds that I was too pessimistic for an optimist to live with.

Krebbs was a bearded man, a platinum blond Jesus with spaniel eyes. He was no close friend of mine. I had met him at a cocktail party where he presented himself as National Chairman of Poets and Painters for Immediate Nuclear War. He begged for shelter, not necessarily bomb proof, and it happened that I had some.

When I returned to my apartment, still twanging with the puzzling spiritual implications of the unclaimed stone angel in Ilium, I found my apartment wrecked by a nihilistic debauch. Krebbs was gone; but, before leaving, he had run up three-hundred-dollars' worth of long-distance calls, set my couch on fire in five places, killed my cat and my avocado tree, and torn the door off my medicine cabinet.

He wrote this poem, in what proved to be excrement, on the yellow linoleum floor of my kitchen:

> I have a kitchen.
> But it is not a complete kitchen.
> I will not be truly gay
> Until I have a
> Dispose-all.

There was another message, written in lipstick in a feminine hand on the wallpaper over my bed. It said: 'No, no, no, said Chicken-licken.'

There was a sign hung around my dead cat's neck. It said, Miaow.

I have not seen Krebbs since. Nonetheless, I sense that he was my *karass*. If he was, he served it as a *wrang-wrang*. A *wrang-wrang*, according to Bokonon, is a person who steers people away from a line of speculation by reducing that line, with the example of the *wrang-wrang*'s own life, to an absurdity.

I might have been vaguely inclined to dismiss the stone angel as meaningless, and to go from there to the meaninglessness of all. But after I saw what Krebbs had done, in particular what he had done to my sweet cat, nihilism was not for me.

Somebody or something did not wish me to be a nihilist. It was Krebbs's mission, whether he knew it or not, to disenchant me with that philosophy. Well done, Mr Krebbs, well done.

## 37  A Modern Major General

And then, one day, one Sunday, I found out where the fugitive from justice, the model-maker, the Great God Jehovah and Beelzebub of bugs in Mason jars was – where Franklin Hoenikker could be found.

He was alive!

The news was in a special supplement to the New York *Sunday Times*. The supplement was a paid ad for a banana republic. On its cover was the profile of the most heart-breakingly beautiful girl I ever hope to see.

Beyond the girl, bulldozers were knocking down palm trees,

making a broad avenue. At the end of the avenue were the steel skeletons of three new buildings.

'The Republic of San Lorenzo,' said the copy on the cover, 'on the move! A healthy, happy, progressive, freedom-loving, beautiful nation makes itself extremely attractive to American investors and tourists alike.'

I was in no hurry to read the contents. The girl on the cover was enough for me – more than enough, since I had fallen in love with her on sight. She was very young and very grave, too – and luminously compassionate and wise.

She was as brown as chocolate. Her hair was like golden flax.

Her name was Mona Aamons Monzano, the cover said. She was the adopted daughter of the dictator of the island.

I opened the supplement, hoping for more pictures of this sublime mongrel Madonna.

I found instead a portrait of the island's dictator, Miguel 'Papa' Monzano, a gorilla in his late seventies.

Next to 'Papa's' portrait was a picture of a narrow-shouldered, fox-faced, immature young man. He wore a snow white military blouse with some sort of jewelled sunburst hanging on it. His eyes were close together; they had circles under them. He had apparently told barbers all his life to shave the sides and back of his head, but to leave the top of his hair alone. He had a wiry pompadour, a sort of cube of hair, marcelled, that arose to an incredible height.

This unattractive child was identified as Major General Franklin Hoenikker, *Minister of Science and Progress in the Republic of San Lorenzo*.

He was twenty-six years old.

## 38 Barracuda Capital of the World

San Lorenzo was fifty miles long and twenty miles wide, I learned from the supplement to the New York *Sunday Times*. Its population was four hundred and fifty thousand souls, '. . . all fiercely dedicated to the ideals of the Free World.'

Its highest point, Mount McCabe, was eleven thousand feet above sea level. Its capital was Bolivar, '. . . a strikingly modern city built on a harbour capable of sheltering the entire United States Navy.' The principal exports were sugar, coffee, bananas, indigo, and handcrafted novelties.

'And sports fishermen recognize San Lorenzo as the unchallenged barracuda capital of the world.'

I wondered how Franklin Hoenikker, who had never even finished high school, had got himself such a fancy job. I found a partial answer in an essay on San Lorenzo that was signed by 'Papa' Monzano.

'Papa' said that Frank was the architect of the 'San Lorenzo Master Plan', which included new roads, rural electrification, sewage-disposal plants, hotels, hospitals, clinics, railroads – the works. And, though the essay was brief and tightly edited, 'Papa' referred to Frank five times as: '. . . the *blood son* of Dr Felix Hoenikker.'

The phrase reeked of cannibalism.

'Papa' plainly felt that Frank was a chunk of the old man's magic meat.

### 39  *Fata Morgana*

A little more light was shed by another essay in the supplement, a florid essay titled, 'What San Lorenzo Has Meant to One American'. It was almost certainly ghost-written. It was signed by Major General Franklin Hoenikker.

In the essay, Frank told of being all alone on a nearly swamped sixty-eight-foot Chris-Craft in the Caribbean. He didn't explain what he was doing on it or how he happened to be alone. He did indicate, though, that his point of departure had been Cuba.

'The luxurious pleasure craft was going down, and my meaningless life with it,' said the essay. 'All I'd eaten for four days was two biscuits and a sea-gull. The dorsal fins of man-eating sharks were cleaving the warm seas around me, and needle-teethed barracuda were making those waters boil.

'I raised my eyes to my Maker, willing to accept whatever His decision might be. And my eyes alighted on a glorious mountain peak above the clouds. Was this Fata Morgana – the cruel deception of a mirage?'

I looked up Fata Morgana at this point in my reading; learned that it was, in fact, a mirage named after Morgan le Fay, a fairy who lived at the bottom of a lake. It was famous for appearing in the Strait of Messina, between Calabria and Sicily. Fata Morgana was poetic crap, in short.

What Frank saw from his sinking pleasure craft was not cruel Fata Morgana, but the peak of Mount McCabe. Gentle seas then nuzzled Frank's pleasure craft to the rocky shores of San Lorenzo, as though God wanted him to go there.

Frank stepped ashore, dry shod, and asked where he was. The essay didn't say so, but the son of a bitch had a piece of *ice-nine* with him – in a thermos jug.

Frank, having no passport, was put in jail in the capital city of Bolivar. He was visited there by 'Papa' Monzano, who wanted to know if it were possible that Frank was a blood relative of the immortal Dr Felix Hoenikker.

'I admitted I was,' said Frank in the essay. 'Since that moment, every door to opportunity in San Lorenzo has been opened wide to me.'

### 40 *House of Hope and Mercy*

As it happened – 'As it was *supposed* to happen,' Bokonon would say – I was assigned by a magazine to do a story in San Lorenzo. The story wasn't to be about 'Papa' Monzano or Frank. It was to be about Julian Castle, an American sugar millionaire who had, at the age of forty, followed the example of Dr Albert Schweitzer by founding a free hospital in a jungle, by devoting his life to miserable folk of another race.

Castle's hospital was called the House of Hope and Mercy in the Jungle. Its jungle was on San Lorenzo, among the wild coffee trees on the northern slope of Mount McCabe.

When I flew to San Lorenzo, Julian Castle was sixty years old.

He had been absolutely unselfish for twenty years.

In his selfish days he had been as familiar to tabloid readers as Tommy Manville, Adolf Hitler, Benito Mussolini, and Barbara Hutton. His fame had rested on lechery, alcoholism, reckless driving, and draft evasion. He had had a dazzling talent for spending millions without increasing mankind's stores of anything but chagrin.

He had been married five times, had produced one son.

The one son, Philip Castle, was the manager and owner of the hotel at which I planned to stay. The hotel was called the

Casa Mona and was named after Mona Aamons Monzano, the blonde Negro on the cover of the supplement to the New York *Sunday Times*. The Casa Mona was brand new; it was one of the three new buildings in the background of the supplement's portrait of Mona.

While I didn't feel that purposeful seas were wafting me to San Lorenzo, I did feel that love was doing the job. The Fata Morgana, the mirage of what it would be like to be loved by Mona Aamons Monzano, had become a tremendous force in my meaningless life. I imagined that she could make me far happier than any woman had so far succeeded in doing.

## 41  A Karass *Built for Two*

The seating on the airplane, bound ultimately for San Lorenzo from Miami, was three and three. As it happened – 'As it was *supposed* to happen' – my seat-mates were Horlick Minton, the new American Ambassador to the Republic of San Lorenzo, and his wife, Claire. They were white-haired, gentle, and frail.

Minton told me that he was a career diplomat, holding the rank of Ambassador for the first time. He and his wife had so far served, he told me, in Bolivia, Chile, Japan, France, Yogoslavia, Egypt, the Union of South Africa, Liberia, and Pakistan.

They were lovebirds. They entertained each other endlessly with little gifts: sights worth seeing out the plane window, amusing or instructive bits from things they read, random recollections of times gone by. They were, I think, a flawless example of what Bokonon calls a *duprass*, which is a *karass* composed of only two persons.

'A true *duprass*,' Bokonon tells us, 'can't be invaded, not even by children born of such a union.'

I exclude the Mintons, therefore, from my own *karass*, from Frank's *karass*, from Newt's *karass*, from Asa Breed's *karass*, from Angela's *karass*, from Lyman Enders Knowles's *karass*, from Sherman Krebbs's *karass*. The Mintons' *karass* was a tidy one, composed of only two.

'I should think you'd be very pleased,' I said to Minton.

'What should I be pleased about?'

'Pleased to have the rank of Ambassador.'

From the pitying way Minton and his wife looked at each other, I gathered that I had said a fat-headed thing. But they humoured me. 'Yes,' winced Minton, 'I'm very pleased.' He smiled wanly. 'I'm *deeply* honoured.'

And so it went with almost every subject I brought up. I couldn't make the Mintons bubble about anything.

For instance: 'I suppose you can speak a lot of languages,' I said.

'Oh, six or seven – between us,' said Minton.

'That must be very gratifying.'

'What must?'

'Being able to speak to people of so many different nationalities.'

'Very gratifying,' said Minton emptily.

'Very gratifying,' said his wife.

And they went back to reading a fat, typewritten manuscript that was spread across the chair arm between them.

'Tell me,' I said a little later, 'in all your wide travels, have you found people everywhere about the same at heart?'

'Hm?' asked Minton.

'Do you find people to be about the same at heart, wherever you go?'

He looked at his wife, making sure she had heard the question, then turned back to me. 'About the same, wherever you go,' he agreed.

'Um,' I said.

Bokonon tells us, incidentally, that members of a *duprass* always die within a week of each other. When it came time for the Mintons to die, they did it within the same second.

## 42 Bicycles for Afghanistan

There was a small saloon in the rear of the plane and I repaired there for a drink. It was there that I met another fellow American, H. Lowe Crosby of Evanston, Illinois, and his wife, Hazel.

They were heavy people, in their fifties. They spoke twangingly. Crosby told me that he owned a bicycle factory in Chicago, that he had had nothing but ingratitude from his employees. He was going to move his business to grateful San Lorenzo.

'You know San Lorenzo well?' I asked.

'This'll be the first time I've ever seen it, but everything I've heard about it I like,' said H. Lowe Crosby. 'They've got discipline. They've got something you can count on from one year to the next. They don't have the government encouraging everybody to be some kind of original pissant nobody ever heard of before.'

'Sir?'

'Christ, back in Chicago, we don't make bicycles any more. It's all human relations now. The eggheads sit around trying to figure out new ways for everybody to be happy. Nobody can get fired, no matter what; and if somebody does accidentally make a bicycle, the union accuses us of cruel and inhuman practices and the government confiscates the bicycle for back taxes and gives it to a blind man in Afghanistan.'

'And you think things will be better in San Lorenzo?'

'I know damn well they will be. The people down there are poor enough and scared enough and ignorant enough to have some common sense!'

Crosby asked me what my name was and what my business was. I told him, and his wife Hazel recognized my name as an Indiana name. She was from Indiana, too.

'My God,' she said, 'are you a *Hoosier*?'

I admitted I was.

'I'm a Hoosier, too,' she crowed. 'Nobody has to be ashamed of being a Hoosier.'

'I'm not,' I said. 'I never knew anybody who was.'

'Hoosiers do all right. Lowe and I've been around the world twice, and everywhere we went we found Hoosiers in charge of everything.'

'That's reassuring.'

'You know the manager of that new hotel in Istanbul?'

'No.'

'He's a Hoosier. And the military-whatever-he-is in Tokyo . . .'

'Attaché,' said her husband.

'He's a Hoosier,' said Hazel. 'And the new Ambassador to Yugoslavia . . .'

'A Hoosier?' I asked.

'Not only him, but the Hollywood Editor of *Life* magazine, too. And that man in Chile . . .'

'A Hoosier, too?'

'You can't go anywhere a *Hoosier* hasn't made his mark,' she said.

'The man who wrote *Ben Hur* was a Hoosier.'

'And James Whitcomb Riley.'

'Are you from Indiana, too?' I asked her husband.

'Nope. I'm a Prairie Stater. "Land of Lincoln", as they say.'

'As far as that goes,' said Hazel triumphantly, 'Lincoln was a Hoosier, too. He grew up in Spencer County.'

'Sure,' I said.

'I don't know what it is about Hoosiers,' said Hazel, 'but they've sure got something. If somebody was to make a list, they'd be amazed.'

'That's true,' I said.

She grasped me firmly by the arm. 'We Hoosiers got to stick together.'

'Right.'

'You call me "Mom".'

'What?'

'Whenever I meet a young Hoosier, I tell them, "You call me *Mom*".'

'Uh huh.'

'Let me hear you say it,' she urged.

'Mom?'

She smiled and let go of my arm. Some piece of clockwork had completed its cycle. My calling Hazel 'Mom' had shut it off, and now Hazel was rewinding it for the next Hoosier to come along.

Hazel's obsession with Hoosiers around the world was a text-book example of a false *karass*, of a seeming team that was meaningless in terms of the ways God gets things done, a text-book example of what Bokonon calls a *granfalloon*. Other examples of *granfalloons* are the Communist party, the Daughters of the American Revolution, the General Electric Company, the International Order of Odd Fellows – and any nation, anytime, anywhere.

As Bokonon invites us to sing along with him:

If you wish to study a *granfalloon*,
Just remove the skin of a toy balloon.

## 43 *The Demonstrator*

H. Lowe Crosby was of the opinion that dictatorships were often very good things. He wasn't a terrible person and he wasn't a fool. It suited him to confront the world with a certain barnyard clownishness, but many of the things he had to say about undisciplined mankind were not only funny but true.

The major point at which his reason and his sense of humour left him was when he approached the question of what people were really supposed to do with their time on Earth.

He believed firmly that they were meant to build bicycles for him.

'I hope San Lorenzo is every bit as good as you've heard it is,' I said.

'I only have to talk to one man to find out if it is or not,' he said. 'When "Papa" Monzano gives his word of honour about anything on that little island, that's it. That's how it is; that's how it'll be.'

'The thing I like,' said Hazel, 'is they all speak English and they're all Christians. That makes things so much easier.'

'You know how they deal with crime down there?' Crosby asked me.

'Nope.'

'They just don't have any crime down there. "Papa" Monzano's made crime so damn unattractive, nobody even thinks about it without getting sick. I heard you can lay a billfold in the middle of a sidewalk and you can come back a week later and it'll be right there, with everything still in it.'

'Um.'

'You know what the punishment is for stealing something?'

'Nope.'

'The hook,' he said. 'No fines, no probation, no thirty days in jail. It's the hook. The hook for stealing, for murder, for arson, for treason, for rape, for being a peeping Tom. Break a law – any damn law at all – and it's the hook. Everybody can understand that, and San Lorenzo is the best-behaved country in the world.'

'What is the hook?'

'They put up a gallows, see? Two posts and a cross beam. And then they take a great big kind of iron fishhook and they hang it down from the cross beam. Then they take somebody who's dumb enough to break the law, and they put the point of the hook in through one side of his belly and out the other and they let him go – and there he hangs, by God, one damn sorry law-breaker.'

'Good God!'

'I don't say it's good,' said Crosby, 'but I don't say it's bad, either. I sometimes wonder if something like that wouldn't clear up juvenile delinquency. Maybe the hook's a little extreme for a democracy. Public hanging's more like it. String up a few teen-age car thieves on lamp posts in front of their houses with signs around their necks saying, "Mama, here's your boy." Do that a few times and I think ignition locks would go the way of the rumble seat and the running board.'

'We saw that thing in the basement of the waxworks in London,' said Hazel.

'What thing?' I asked her.

'The hook. Down in the Chamber of Horrors in the basement; they had a wax person hanging from the hook. It looked so real I wanted to throw up.'

'Harry Truman didn't look anything like Harry Truman,' said Crosby.

'Pardon me?'

'In the waxworks,' said Crosby. 'The statue of Truman didn't really look like him.'

'Most of them did, though,' said Hazel.

'Was it anybody in particular hanging from the hook?' I asked her.

'I don't think so. It was just somebody.'

'Just a demonstrator?' I asked.

'Yeah. There was a black velvet curtain in front of it and you had to pull the curtain back to see. And there was a note pinned to the curtain that said children weren't supposed to look.'

'But kids did,' said Crosby. 'There were kids down there, and they all looked.'

'A sign like that is just catnip to kids,' said Hazel.

'How did the kids react when they saw the person on the hook?' I asked.

'Oh,' said Hazel, 'they reacted just about the way the grown-ups did. They just looked at it and didn't say anything, just moved on to see what the next thing was.'

'What was the next thing?'

'It was an iron chair a man had been roasted alive in,' said Crosby. 'He was roasted for murdering his son.'

'Only, after they roasted him,' Hazel recalled blandly, 'they found out he hadn't murdered his son after all.'

## 44 Communist Sympathizers

When I again took my seat beside the *duprass* of Claire and Horlick Minton, I had some new information about them. I got it from the Crosbys.

The Crosbys didn't know Minton, but they knew his reputation. They were indignant about his appointment as Ambassador. They told me that Minton had once been fired by the State

Department for his softness towards communism, and that communist dupes or worse had had him reinstated.

'Very pleasant little saloon back there,' I said to Minton as I sat down.

'Hm?' He and his wife were still reading the manuscript that lay between them.

'Nice bar back there.'

'Good. I'm glad.'

The two read on, apparently uninterested in talking to me. And then Minton turned to me suddenly, with a bitter-sweet smile, and he demanded, 'Who was he, anyway?'

'Who was who?'

'The man you were talking to in the bar. We went back there for a drink, and, when we were just outside, we heard you and a man talking. The man was talking very loudly. He said I was a communist sympathizer.'

'A bicycle manufacturer named H. Lowe Crosby,' I said. I felt myself reddening.

'I was fired for pessimism. Communism had nothing to do with it.'

'I got him fired,' said his wife. 'The only piece of real evidence produced against him was a letter I wrote to the New York *Times* from Pakistan.'

'What did it say?'

'It said a lot of things,' she said, 'because I was very upset about how Americans couldn't imagine what it was like to be something else, to be something else and proud of it.'

'I see.'

'But there was one sentence they kept coming back to again and again in the loyalty hearing,' sighed Minton. '"Americans",' he said, quoting his wife's letter to the *Times*, '"are forever searching for love in forms it never takes, in places it can never be. It must have something to do with the vanished frontier."'

## 45 Why Americans Are Hated

Claire Minton's letter to the *Times* was published during the worst of the era of Senator McCarthy, and her husband was fired twelve hours after the letter was printed.

'What was so awful about the letter?' I asked.

'The highest possible form of treason,' said Minton, 'is to say that Americans aren't loved wherever they go, whatever they do. Claire tried to make the point that American foreign policy should recognize hate rather than imagine love.'

'I guess Americans *are* hated a lot of places.'

'*People* are hated a lot of places. Claire pointed out in her letter that Americans, in being hated, were simply paying the normal penalty for being people, and that they were foolish to think they should somehow be exempted from that penalty. But the loyalty board didn't pay any attention to that. All they knew was that Claire and I both felt that Americans were unloved.'

'Well, I'm glad the story had a happy ending.'

'Hm?' said Minton.

'It finally came out all right,' I said. 'Here you are on your way to an embassy all of your own.'

Minton and his wife exchanged another of those pitying *duprass* glances. Then Minton said to me, 'Yes. The pot of gold at the end of the rainbow is ours.'

## 46 *The Bokononist Method for Handling Caesar*

I talked to the Mintons about the legal status of Franklin Hoenikker, who was, after all, not only a big shot in 'Papa' Monzano's government, but a fugitive from United States justice.

'That's all been written off,' said Minton. 'He isn't a United States citizen any more, and he seems to be doing good things where he is, so that's that.'

'He gave up his citizenship?'

'Anybody who declares allegiance to a foreign state or serves in its armed forces or accepts employment in its government loses his citizenship. Read your passport. You can't lead the sort of funny-paper international romance that Frank has led and still have Uncle Sam for a mother chicken.'

'Is he well liked in San Lorenzo?'

Minton weighed in his hands the manuscript he and his wife had been reading. 'I don't know yet. This book says not.'

'What book is that?'

'It's the only scholarly book ever written about San Lorenzo.'

'*Sort* of scholarly,' said Claire.

'*Sort* of scholarly,' echoed Minton. 'It hasn't been published yet. This is one of five copies.' He handed it to me, inviting me to read as much as I liked.

I opened the book to its title page and found that the name of the book was *San Lorenzo: The Land, the History, the People*. The author was Philip Castle, the son of Julian Castle, the hotel-keeping son of the great altruist I was on my way to see.

I let the book fall open where it would. As it happened, it fell open to the chapter about the island's outlawed holy man, Bokonon.

There was a quotation from *The Books of Bokonon* on the page before me. Those words leapt from the page and into my mind, and they were welcomed there.

The words were a paraphrase of the suggestion by Jesus: 'Render therefore unto Caesar the things which are Caesar's.'

Bokonon's paraphrase was this:

'Pay no attention to Caesar. Caesar doesn't have the slightest idea what's *really* going on.'

## 47 Dynamic Tension

I became so absorbed in Philip Castle's book that I didn't even look up from it when we put down for ten minutes in San Juan, Puerto Rico. I didn't even look up when somebody behind me whispered, thrilled, that a midget had come aboard.

A little while later I looked around for the midget, but could not see him. I did see, right in front of Hazel and H. Lowe Crosby, a horse-faced woman with platinum blonde hair, a woman new to the passenger list. Next to hers was a seat that appeared to be empty, a seat that might well have sheltered a midget without my seeing even the top of his head.

But it was San Lorenzo – the land, the history, the people – that intrigued me then, so I looked no harder for the midget. Midgets are, after all, diversions for silly or quiet times, and I was serious and excited about Bokonon's theory of what he called 'Dynamic Tension', his sense of a priceless equilibrium between good and evil.

When I first saw the term 'Dynamic Tension' in Philip Castle's book, I laughed what I imagined to be a superior laugh. The term was a favourite of Bokonon's, according to young Castle's book, and I supposed that I knew something that

Bokonon didn't know: that the term was one vulgarized by Charles Atlas, a mail-order muscle-builder.

As I learned when I read on, briefly, Bokonon knew exactly who Charles Atlas was. Bokonon was, in fact, an alumnus of his muscle-building school.

It was the belief of Charles Atlas that muscles could be built without bar bells or spring exercisers, could be built by simply pitting one set of muscles against another.

It was the belief of Bokonon that good societies could be built only by pitting good against evil, and by keeping the tension between the two high at all times.

And, in Castle's book, I read my first Bokononist poem, or 'Calypso'. It went like this:

> 'Papa' Monzano, he's so very bad,
> But without bad 'Papa' I would be so sad;
> Because without 'Papa's' badness,
> Tell me, if you would,
> How could wicked old Bokonon
> Ever, ever look good?

## 48 *Just Like Saint Augustine*

Bokonon, I learned from Castle's book, was born in 1891. He was a Negro, born an Episcopalian and a British subject on the island of Tobago.

He was christened Lionel Boyd Johnson.

He was the youngest of six children, born to a wealthy family. His family's wealth derived from the discovery by Bokonon's grandfather of one quarter of a million dollars in buried pirate treasure, presumably a treasure of Blackbeard, of Edward Teach.

Blackbeard's treasure was reinvested by Bokonon's family in asphalt, copra, cacao, livestock, and poultry.

Young Lionel Boyd Johnson was educated in Episcopal schools, did well as a student, and was more interested in ritual than most. As a youth, for all his interest in the outward trappings of organized religion, he seems to have been a carouser, for he invites us to sing along with him in his 'Fourteenth Calypso':

> When I was young,
> I was so gay and mean,
> And I drank and chased the girls
> Just like young St Augustine.
> Saint Augustine,
> He got to be a saint.
> So, if I get to be one, also,
> Please, Mama, don't you faint.

## 49 A Fish Pitched Up by an Angry Sea

Lionel Boyd Johnson was intellectually ambitious enough, in 1911, to sail alone from Tobago to London in a sloop named the *Lady's Slipper*. His purpose was to gain a higher education.

He enrolled in the London School of Economics and Political Science.

His education was interrupted by the First World War. He enlisted in the infantry, fought with distinction, was commissioned in the field, was mentioned four times in dispatches.

He was gassed in the second Battle of Ypres, was hospitalized for two years, and then discharged.

And he set sail for home, for Tobago, alone in the *Lady's Slipper* again.

When only eight miles from home, he was stopped and searched by a German submarine, the *U-99*. He was taken prisoner, and his little vessel was used by the Huns for target practice. While still surfaced, the submarine was surprised and captured by the British destroyer, the *Raven*.

Johnson and the Germans were taken on board the destroyer and the *U-99* was sunk.

The *Raven* was bound for the Mediterranean, but it never got there. It lost its steering; it could only wallow helplessly or make grand, clockwise circles. It came to rest at last in the Cape Verde Islands.

Johnson stayed in those islands for eight months, awaiting some sort of transportation to the Western Hemisphere.

He got a job at last as a crewman on a fishing vessel that was carrying illegal immigrants to New Bedford, Massachusetts. The vessel was blown ashore at Newport, Rhode Island.

By that time Johnson had developed a conviction that something was trying to get him somewhere for some reason. So he stayed in Newport for a while to see if he had a destiny there. He worked as a gardener and carpenter on the famous Rumfoord Estate.

During that time, he glimpsed many distinguished guests of the Rumfoords, among them J. P. Morgan, General John J. Pershing, Franklin Delano Roosevelt, Enrico Caruso, Warren Gamaliel Harding, and Harry Houdini. And it was during that time that the First World War came to an end, having killed ten million persons and wounded twenty million, Johnson among them.

When the war ended, the young rakehell of the Rumfoord

family, Remington Rumfoord, IV, proposed to sail his steam yacht, the *Scheherazade*, around the world, visiting Spain, France, Italy, Greece, Egypt, India, China, and Japan. He invited Johnson to accompany him as first mate, and Johnson agreed.

Johnson saw many wonders of the world on the voyage.

The *Scheherazade* was rammed in a fog in Bombay harbour, and only Johnson survived. He stayed in India for two years, becoming a follower of Mohandas K. Gandhi. He was arrested for leading groups that protested against British rule by lying down on railroad tracks. When his jail term was over, he was shipped at Crown expense to his home in Tobago.

There, he built another schooner, which he called the *Lady's Slipper II*.

And he sailed her about the Caribbean, an idler, still seeking the storm that would drive him ashore on what was unmistakably his destiny.

In 1922, he sought shelter from a hurricane in Port-au-Prince, Haiti, which country was then occupied by United States Marines.

Johnson was approached there by a brilliant, self-educated, idealistic Marine deserter, Earl McCabe. McCabe was a corporal. He had just stolen his company's recreation fund. He offered Johnson five hundred dollars for transportation to Miami.

The two set sail for Miami.

But a gale hounded the schooner on to the rocks of San Lorenzo. The boat went down. Johnson and McCabe, absolutely naked, managed to swim ashore. As Bokonon himself reports the adventure:

> A fish pitched up
> By the angry sea,
> I gasped on land,
> And I became me.

He was enchanted by the mystery of coming ashore naked on an unfamiliar island. He resolved to let the adventure run its full course, resolved to see just how far a man might go, emerging naked from salt water.

It was a rebirth for him:

> Be like a baby,
> The Bible say,
> So I stay like a baby
> To this very day.

How he came by the name of Bokonon was very simple. 'Bokonon' was the pronunciation given the name Johnson in the island's English dialect.

As for that dialect . . .

The dialect of San Lorenzo is both easy to understand and difficult to write down. I say it is easy to understand, but I speak only for myself. Others have found it as incomprehensible as Basque, so my understanding of it may be telepathic.

Philip Castle, in his book, gave a phonetic demonstration of the dialect and caught its flavour very well. He chose for his sample the San Lorenzan version of 'Twinkle, Twinkle, Little Star'.

In American English, one version of that immortal poem goes like this:

> Twinkle, twinkle, little star,
> How I wonder what you are,
> Shining in the sky so bright,
> Like a tea tray in the night,
> Twinkle, twinkle, little star,
> How I wonder what you are.

In San Lorenzan dialect, according to Castle, the same poem went like this:

> *Tsvent-kiul, tsvent-kiul, lett-pool store,*
> *Ko jy tsvantoor bat voo yore.*
> *Put-shinik on lo shee zo brath,*
> *Kam oon teetron on lo nath,*
> *Tsvent-kiul, tsvent-kiul, lett-pool store,*
> *Ko jy tsvantoor bat voo yore.*

Shortly after Johnson became Bokonon, incidentally, the lifeboat of his shattered ship was found on shore. That boat was later painted gold and made the bed of the island's chief executive.

'There is a legend, made up by Bokonon,' Philip Castle wrote in his book, 'that the golden boat will sail again when the end of the world is near.'

## 50 A Nice Midget

My reading of the life of Bokonon was interrupted by H. Lowe Crosby's wife, Hazel. She was standing in the aisle next to me. 'You'll never believe it,' she said, 'but I just found two more Hoosiers on this airplane.'

'I'll be damned.'

'They weren't born Hoosiers, but they *live* there now. They live in Indianapolis.'

'Very interesting.'

'You want to meet them?'

'You think I should?'

The question baffled her. 'They're your fellow Hoosiers.'

'What are their names?'

'Her name is Conners and his name is Hoenikker. They're brother and sister, and he's a midget. He's a nice midget, though.' She winked. 'He's a smart little thing.'

'Does he call you Mom?'

'I almost asked him to. And then I stopped, and I wondered if maybe it wouldn't be rude to ask a midget to do that.'

'Nonsense.'

### 51  O.K., Mom

So I went aft to talk to Angela Hoenikker Conners and little Newton Hoenikker, members of my *karass*.

Angela was the horse-faced platinum blonde I had noticed earlier.

Newt was a very tiny young man indeed, though not grotesque. He was as nicely scaled as Gulliver among the Brobdingnagians, and as shrewdly watchful, too.

He held a glass of champagne, which was included in the price of his ticket. That glass was to him what a fishbowl would have been to a normal man, but he drank from it with elegant ease – as though he and the glass could not have been better matched.

The little son of a bitch had a crystal of *ice-nine* in a thermos bottle in his luggage, and so did his miserable sister, while under us was God's own amount of water, the Caribbean Sea.

When Hazel had got all the pleasure she could from introducing Hoosiers to Hoosiers, she left us alone. 'Remember,' she said as she left us, 'from now on, call me *Mom*.'

'O.K., Mom,' I said.

'O.K., Mom,' said Newt. His voice was fairly high, in keeping with his little larynx. But he managed to make that voice distinctly masculine.

Angela persisted in treating Newt like an infant – and he forgave her for it with an amiable grace I would have thought impossible for one so small.

Newt and Angela remembered me, remembered the letters I'd written, and invited me to take the empty seat in their group of three.

Angela apologized to me for never having answered my letters.

'I couldn't think of anything to say that would interest anybody reading a book. I could have made up something about that day, but I didn't think you'd want that. Actually, the day was just like a regular day.'

'Your brother here wrote me a very good letter.'

Angela was surprised. 'Newt did? How could Newt remember anything?' She turned to him. 'Honey, you don't remember anything about that day, do you? You were just a baby.'

'I remember,' he said mildly.

'I wish I'd *seen* the letter.' She implied that Newt was still too immature to deal directly with the outside world. Angela was a God-awfully insensitive woman, with no feeling for what smallness meant to Newt.

'Honey, you should have showed me that letter,' she scolded.

'Sorry,' said Newt. 'I didn't think.'

'I might as well tell you,' Angela said to me, 'Dr Breed told me I wasn't supposed to cooperate with you. He said you weren't interested in giving a fair picture of Father.' She showed me that she didn't like me for that.

I placated her some by telling her that the book would probably never be done anyway, that I no longer had a clear idea of what it would or should mean.

'Well, if you ever *do* do the book, you better make Father a saint, because that's what he was.'

I promised that I would do my best to paint that picture. I asked if she and Newt were bound for a family reunion with Frank in San Lorenzo.

'Frank's getting married,' said Angela. 'We're going to the engagement party.'

'Oh? Who's the lucky girl?'

'I'll show you,' said Angela, and she took from her purse a billfold that contained a sort of plastic accordion. In each of the accordion's pleats was a photograph. Angela flipped through the photographs, giving me glimpses of Little Newt on a Cape Cod beach, of Dr Felix Hoenikker accepting his Nobel Prize, of Angela's own homely twin girls, of Frank flying a model plane on the end of a string.

And then she showed me a picture of the girl Frank was going to marry.

She might, with equal effect, have struck me in the groin.

The picture she showed me was of Mona Aamons Monzano, the woman I loved.

## 52 No Pain

Once Angela had opened her plastic accordion, she was reluctant to close it until someone had looked at every photograph.

'There are the people I love,' she declared.

So I looked at the people she loved. What she had trapped in plexiglass, what she had trapped like fossil beetles in amber, were the images of a large part of our *karass*. There wasn't a *granfallooner* in the collection.

There were many photographs of Dr Hoenikker, father of a

bomb, father of three children, father of *ice-nine*. He was a little person, the purported sire of a midget and a giantess.

My favourite picture of the old man in Angela's fossil collection showed him all bundled up for winter, in an overcoat, scarf, galoshes, and a wool knit cap with a big pom-pom on the crown.

This picture, Angela told me, with a catch in her throat, had been taken in Hyannis just about three hours before the old man died. A newspaper photographer had recognized the seeming Christmas elf for the great man he was.

'Did your father die in the hospital?'

'Oh, no! He died in our cottage, in a big white wicker chair facing the sea. Newt and Frank had gone walking down the beach in the snow . . .'

'It was a very warm snow,' said Newt. 'It was almost like walking through orange blossoms. It was very strange. Nobody was in any of the other cottages . . .'

'Ours was the only one with heat,' said Angela.

'Nobody within miles,' recalled Newt wonderingly, 'and Frank and I came across this big black dog out on the beach, a Labrador retriever. We threw sticks into the ocean and he brought them back.'

'I'd gone back into the village for more Christmas tree bulbs,' said Angela. 'We always had a tree.'

'Did your father enjoy having a Christmas tree?'

'He never said,' said Newt.

'I think he liked it,' said Angela. 'He just wasn't very demonstrative. Some people aren't.'

'And some people are,' said Newt. He gave a small shrug.

'Anyway,' said Angela, 'when we got back home, we found him in the chair.' She shook her head. 'I don't think he suffered any. He just looked asleep. He couldn't have looked like that if there'd been the least bit of pain.'

She left out an interesting part of the story. She left out the fact that it was on that same Christmas Eve that she and Frank and little Newt had divided up the old man's *ice-nine*.

## 53 *The President of Fabri-Tek*

Angela encouraged me to go on looking at snapshots.

'That's me, if you can believe it.' She showed me an adolescent girl six feet tall. She was holding a clarinet in the picture, wearing the marching uniform of the Ilium High School band. Her hair was tucked up under a bandsman's hat. She was smiling with shy good cheer.

And then Angela, a woman to whom God had given virtually nothing with which to catch a man, showed me a picture of her husband.

'So that's Harrison C. Conners.' I was stunned. Her husband was a strikingly handsome man, and looked as though he knew it. He was a snappy dresser, and had the lazy rapture of a Don Juan about the eyes.

'What – what does he do?' I asked.

'He's president of Fabri-Tek.'

'Electronics?'

'I couldn't tell you, even if I knew. It's all very secret government work.'

'Weapons?'

'Well, war anyway.'

'How did you happen to meet?'

'He used to work as a laboratory assistant to Father,' said Angela. 'Then he went out to Indianapolis and started Fabri-Tek.'

'So your marriage to him was a happy ending to a long romance?'

'No. I didn't even know he knew I was alive. I used to think he was nice, but he never paid any attention to me until after Father died.

'One day he came through Ilium. I was sitting around that big old house, thinking my life was over . . .' She spoke of the awful days and weeks that followed her father's death. 'Just me and little Newt in that big old house. Frank had disappeared, and the ghosts were making ten times as much noise as Newt and I were. I'd given my whole life to taking care of Father, driving him to and from work, bundling him up when it was cold, unbundling him when it was hot, making him eat, paying his bills. Suddenly, there wasn't anything for me to do. I'd never had any close friends, didn't have a soul to turn to but Newt.

'And then,' she continued, 'there was a knock on the door – and there stood Harrison Conners. He was the most beautiful thing I'd ever seen. He came in, and we talked about Father's last days and about old times in general.'

Angela almost cried now.

'Two weeks later, we were married.'

## 54 *Communists, Nazis, Royalists, Parachutists, and Draft Dodgers*

Returning to my own seat in the plane, feeling far shabbier for having lost Mona Aamons Monzano to Frank, I resumed my reading of Philip Castle's manuscript.

I looked up *Monzano, Mona Aamons* in the index, and was told by the index to see *Aamons, Mona*.

So I saw *Aamons, Mona*, and found almost as many page references as I'd found after the name of 'Papa' Monzano himself.

And after *Aamons, Mona* came *Aamons, Nestor*. So I turned to the few pages that had to do with Nestor, and learned that he was Mona's father, a native Finn, an architect.

Nestor Aamons was captured by the Russians, then liberated by the Germans during the Second World War. He was not returned home by his liberators, but was forced to serve in a *Wehrmacht* engineer unit that was sent to fight the Yugoslav partisans. He was captured by Chetniks, royalist Serbian partisans, and then by communist partisans who attacked the Chetniks. He was liberated by Italian parachutists who surprised the communists, and he was shipped to Italy.

The Italians put him to work designing fortifications for Sicily. He stole a fishing boat in Sicily, and reached neutral Portugal.

While there, he met an American draft dodger named Julian Castle.

Castle, upon learning that Aamons was an architect, invited him to come with him to the island of San Lorenzo and to design for him a hospital to be called the House of Hope and Mercy in the Jungle.

Aamons accepted. He designed the hospital, married a native woman named Celia, fathered a perfect daughter, and died.

## 55 Never Index Your Own Book

As for the life of *Aamons, Mona*, the index itself gave a jangling, surrealistic picture of the many conflicting forces that had been brought to bear on her and of her dismayed reactions to them.

'*Aamons, Mona:*' the index said, 'adopted by Monzano in order to boost Monzano's popularity, 194–9, 216n.; childhood in compound of House of Hope and Mercy, 63–81; childhood romance with P. Castle, 72 f; death of father, 89 ff; death of mother, 92 f; embarrassed by role as national erotic symbol, 80, 95 f, 166n., 209, 247n., 400–406, 566n., 678; engaged to P. Castle, 193; essential naïveté, 67–71, 80, 95 f, 116 n., 209, 274 n., 400–406, 566n., 678; lives with Bokonon, 92–8, 196–7; poems about, 2 n., 26, 114, 119, 311, 316, 477 n., 501, 507, 555 n., 689, 718 ff, 799 ff, 800 n., 841, 846 ff, 908 n., 971, 974; poems by, 89, 92, 193; returns to Monzano, 199; returns to Bokonon, 197; runs away from Bokonon, 199; runs away from Monzano, 197; tries to make self ugly in order to stop erotic symbol to islanders, 90, 95 f, 116, 209, 247 n., 400–406, 566 n., 678; tutored by Bokonon, 63–80; writes letter to United Nations, 200; xylophone virtuoso, 71.'

I showed this index entry to the Mintons, asking them if they didn't think it was an enchanting biography in itself, a biography of a reluctant goddess of love. I got an unexpectedly expert answer, as one does in life sometimes. It appeared that Claire Minton, in her time, had been a professional indexer. I had never heard of such a profession before.

She told me that she had put her husband through college years before with her earnings as an indexer, that the earnings had been good, and that few people could index well.

She said that indexing was a thing that only the most amateur-ish author undertook to do for his own book. I asked her what she thought of Philip Castle's job.

'Flattering to the author, insulting to the reader,' she said. 'In a hyphenated word,' she observed, with the shrewd amiability of an expert, ' *"self-indulgent"*. I'm always embarrassed when I see an index an author has made of his own work.'

'Embarrassed?'

'It's a revealing thing, an author's index of his own work,' she informed me. 'It's a shameless exhibition – to the *trained* eye.'

'She can read character from an index,' said her husband.

'Oh?' I said. 'What can you tell about Philip Castle?'

She smiled faintly. 'Things I'd better not tell strangers.'

'Sorry.'

'He's obviously in love with this Mona Aamons Monzano,' she said.

'That's true of every man in San Lorenzo, I gather.'

'He has mixed feelings about his father,' she said.

'That's true of every man on earth.' I egged her on gently.

'He's insecure.'

'What mortal isn't?' I demanded. I didn't know it then, but that was a very Bokononist thing to demand.

'He'll never marry her.'

'Why not?'

'I've said all I'm going to say,' she said.

'I'm gratified to meet an indexer who respects the privacy of others.'

'Never index your own book,' she stated.

A *duprass*, Bokonon tells us, is a valuable instrument for gaining and developing, in the privacy of an interminable love affair, insights that are queer but true. The Mintons' cunning exploration of indexes was surely a case in point. A *duprass*, Bokonon tells us, is also a sweetly conceited establishment. The Mintons' establishment was no exception.

Sometime later, Ambassador Minton and I met in the aisle of the airplane, away from his wife, and he showed that it was important to him that I respect what his wife could find out from indexes.

'You know why Castle will never marry the girl, even though he loves her, even though she loves him, even though they grew up together?' he whispered.

'No, sir, I don't.'

'Because he's a homosexual,' whispered Minton. 'She can tell that from an index, too.'

## 56 A Self-supporting Squirrel Cage

When Lionel Boyd Johnson and Corporal Earl McCabe were washed up naked onto the shore of San Lorenzo, I read, they were greeted by persons far worse off than they. The people of San Lorenzo had nothing but diseases, which they were at a loss to treat or even name. By contrast, Johnson and McCabe had the glittering treasures of literacy, ambition, curiosity, gall, irreverence, health, humour, and considerable information about the outside world.

From the 'Calypsos' again:

> Oh, a very sorry people, yes,
> Did I find here.
> Oh, they had no music,
> And they had no beer.
> And, oh, everywhere
> Where they tried to perch
> Belonged to Castle Sugar, Incorporated,
> Or the Catholic church.

This statement of the property situation in San Lorenzo in 1922 is entirely accurate, according to Philip Castle. Castle Sugar was founded, as it happened, by Philip Castle's great-grandfather. In 1922, it owned every piece of arable land on the island.

'Castle Sugar's San Lorenzo operations,' wrote young Castle, 'never showed a profit. But, by paying labourers nothing for their labour, the company managed to break even year after year, making just enough money to pay the salaries of the workers' tormentors.

'The form of government was anarchy, save in limited situations wherein Castle Sugar wanted to own something or to get something done. In such situations the form of government was feudalism. The nobility was composed of Castle Sugar's plantation bosses, who were heavily armed white men from the outside world. The knighthood was composed of big natives who, for small gifts and silly privileges, would kill or wound or torture on command. The spiritual needs of the people caught in this demoniacal squirrel cage were taken care of by a handful of butterball priests.

'The San Lorenzo Cathedral, dynamited in 1923, was generally regarded as one of the man-made wonders of the New World,' wrote Castle.

## 57 *The Queasy Dream*

That Corporal McCabe and Johnson were able to take command of San Lorenzo was not a miracle in any sense. Many people had taken over San Lorenzo – had invariably found it lightly held. The reason was simple: God, in His Infinite Wisdom, had made the island worthless.

Hernando Cortes was the first man to have his sterile conquest of San Lorenzo recorded on paper. Cortes and his men came ashore for fresh water in 1519, named the island, claimed it for Emperor Charles the Fifth, and never returned. Subsequent expeditions came for gold and diamonds and rubies and spices, found none, burned a few natives for entertainment and heresy, and sailed on.

'When France claimed San Lorenzo in 1682,' wrote Castle, 'no Spaniards complained. When Denmark claimed San Lorenzo in 1699, no Frenchmen complained. When the Dutch claimed San Lorenzo in 1704, no Danes complained. When England claimed

San Lorenzo in 1706, no Dutchmen complained. When Spain reclaimed San Lorenzo in 1720, no Englishmen complained. When, in 1786, African Negroes took command of a British slave ship, ran it ashore on San Lorenzo, and proclaimed San Lorenzo an independent nation, an empire with an emperor, in fact, no Spaniards complained.

'The emperor was Tum-bumwa, the only person who ever regarded the island as being worth defending. A maniac, Tum-bumwa caused to be erected the San Lorenzo Cathedral and the fantastic fortifications on the north shore of the island, fortifications within which the private residence of the so-called President of the Republic now stands.

'The fortifications have never been attacked, nor has any sane man ever proposed any reason why they should be attacked. They have never defended anything. Fourteen hundred persons are said to have died while building them. Of these fourteen hundred, about half are said to have been executed in public for sub-standard zeal.'

Castle Sugar came into San Lorenzo in 1916, during the sugar boom of the First World War. There was no government at all. The company imagined that even the clay and gravel fields of San Lorenzo could be tilled profitably, with the price of sugar so high. No one complained.

When McCabe and Johnson arrived in 1922 and announced that they were placing themselves in charge, Castle Sugar withdrew flaccidly, as though from a queasy dream.

## 58  *Tyranny with a Difference*

'There was at least one quality of the new conquerors of San Lorenzo that was really new,' wrote young Castle. 'McCabe and Johnson dreamed of making San Lorenzo a Utopia.

'To this end, McCabe overhauled the economy and the laws.

'Johnson designed a new religion.'

Castle quoted the 'Calypsos' again:

> I wanted all things
> To seem to make some sense,
> So we all could be happy, yes,
> Instead of tense.
> And I made up lies
> So that they all fit nice,
> And I made this sad world
> A par-a-dise.

There was a tug at my coat sleeve as I read. I looked up.

Little Newt Hoenikker was standing in the aisle next to me. 'I thought maybe you'd like to go back to the bar,' he said, 'and hoist a few.'

So we did hoist and topple a few, and Newt's tongue was loosened enough to tell me some things about Zinka, his Russian midget dancer friend. Their love nest, he told me, had been in his father's cottage on Cape Cod.

'I may not ever have a marriage, but at least I've had a honeymoon.'

He told me of idyllic hours he and his Zinka had spent in each other's arms, cradled in Felix Hoenikker's old white wicker chair, the chair that faced the sea.

And Zinka would dance for him. 'Imagine a woman dancing just for me.'

'I can see you have no regrets.'

'She broke my heart. I didn't like that much. But that was the price. In this world, you get what you pay for.'

He proposed a gallant toast. 'Sweethearts and wives,' he cried.

## 59 *Fasten Your Seat Belts*

I was in the bar with Newt and H. Lowe Crosby and a couple of strangers, when San Lorenzo was sighted. Crosby was talking about pissants. 'You know what I mean by a pissant?'

'I know the term,' I said, 'but it obviously doesn't have the ding-a-ling associations for me that it has for you.'

Crosby was in his cups and had the drunkard's illusion that he could speak frankly, provided he spoke affectionately. He spoke frankly and affectionately of Newt's size, something nobody else in the bar had so far commented on.

'I don't mean a little feller like this.' Crosby hung a ham hand on Newt's shoulder. 'It isn't size that makes a man a pissant. It's the way he thinks. I've seen men four times as big as this little feller here, and they were pissants. And I've seen little fellers – well, not this little actually, but pretty damn little, by God – and I'd call them real men.'

'Thanks,' said Newt pleasantly, not even glancing at the monstrous hand on his shoulder. Never had I seen a human being better adjusted to such a humiliating physical handicap. I shuddered with admiration.

'You were talking about pissants,' I said to Crosby, hoping to get the weight of his hand off Newt.

'Damn right I was.' Crosby straightened up.

'You haven't told us what a pissant is yet,' I said.

'A pissant is somebody who thinks he's so damn smart, he never can keep his mouth shut. No matter what anybody says, he's got to argue with it. You say you like something, and, by God, he'll tell you why you're wrong to like it. A pissant does his best to make you feel like a boob all the time. No matter what you say, he knows better.'

'Not a very attractive characteristic,' I suggested.

'My daughter wanted to marry a pissant once,' said Crosby darkly.

'Did she?'

'I squashed him like a bug.' Crosby hammered on the bar, remembering things the pissant had said and done. 'Jesus!' he said, 'we've all been to college!' His gaze lit on Newt again. 'You go to college?'

'Cornell,' said Newt.

'Cornell!' cried Crosby gladly. 'My God, I went to Cornell.'

'So did he.' Newt nodded at me.

'Three Cornellians – all in the same plane!' said Crosby, and we had another *granfalloon* festival on our hands.

When it subsided some, Crosby asked Newt what he did.

'I paint.'

'Houses?'

'Pictures.'

'I'll be damned,' said Crosby.

'Return to your seats and fasten your seat belts, please,' warned the airline hostess. 'We're over Monzano Airport, Bolivar, San Lorenzo.'

'Christ! Now wait just a Goddamn minute here,' said Crosby, looking down at Newt. 'All of a sudden I realize you've got a name I've heard before.'

'My father was the father of the atom bomb.' Newt didn't

93

say Felix Hoenikker was *one* of the fathers. He said Felix was *the* father.

'Is that so?' asked Crosby.

'That's so.'

'I was thinking about something else,' said Crosby. He had to think hard. 'Something about a dancer.'

'I think we'd better get back to our seats,' said Newt, tightening some.

'Something about a Russian dancer.' Crosby was sufficiently addled by booze to see no harm in thinking out loud. 'I remember an editorial about how maybe the dancer was a spy.'

'Please, gentlemen,' said the stewardess, 'you really must get back to your seats and fasten your belts.'

Newt looked up at H. Lowe Crosby innocently. 'You sure the name was Hoenikker?' And, in order to eliminate any chance of mistaken identity, he spelled the name for Crosby.

'I could be wrong,' said H. Lowe Crosby.

## 60  An Underprivileged Nation

The island, seen from the air, was an amazingly regular rectangle. Cruel and useless stone needles were thrust up from the sea. They sketched a circle around it.

At the south end of the island was the port city of Bolivar.

It was the only city.

It was the capital.

It was built on a marshy table. The runways of Monzano Airport were on its waterfront.

Mountains arose abruptly to the north of Bolivar, crowding the remainder of the island with their brutal humps. They were called the Sangre de Cristo Mountains, but they looked like pigs at a trough to me.

Bolivar had had many names: Caz-ma-caz-ma, Santa Maria, Saint Louis, Saint George, and Port Glory among them. It was given its present name by Johnson and McCabe in 1922, was named in honour of Simón Bolívar, the great Latin-American idealist and hero.

When Johnson and McCabe came upon the city, it was built of twigs, tin, crates, and mud – rested on the catacombs of a trillion happy scavengers, catacombs in a sour mash of slop, feculence, and slime.

That was pretty much the way I found it, too, except for the new architectural false face along the waterfront.

Johnson and McCabe had failed to raise the people from misery and muck.

'Papa' Monzano had failed, too.

Everybody was bound to fail, for San Lorenzo was as unproductive as an equal area in the Sahara or the Polar Ice Cap.

At the same time, it had as dense a population as could be found anywhere, India and China not excluded. There were four hundred and fifty inhabitants for each uninhabitable square mile.

'During the idealistic phase of McCabe's and Johnson's reorganization of San Lorenzo, it was announced that the country's total income would be divided among all adult persons in equal shares,' wrote Philip Castle. 'The first and only time this was tried, each share came to between six and seven dollars.'

## 61 *What a Corporal Was Worth*

In the customs shed at Monzano Airport, we were all required to submit to a luggage inspection, and to convert what money we intended to spend in San Lorenzo into the local currency, into *Corporals*, which 'Papa' Monzano insisted were worth fifty American cents.

The shed was neat and new, but plenty of signs had already been slapped on the walls, higgledy-piggledy.

ANYBODY CAUGHT PRACTISING BOKONONISM IN SAN LORENZO, said one, WILL DIE ON THE HOOK!

Another poster featured a picture of Bokonon, a scrawny old coloured man who was smoking a cigar. He looked clever and kind and amused.

Under the picture were the words: WANTED DEAD OR ALIVE, 10,000 CORPORALS REWARD!

I took a closer look at that poster and found reproduced at the bottom of it some sort of police identification form Bokonon had had to fill out way back in 1929. It was reproduced, apparently, to show Bokonon hunters what his fingerprints and handwriting were like.

But what interested me were some of the words Bokonon had chosen to put into the blanks in 1929. Wherever possible, he had taken the cosmic view, had taken into consideration, for instance, such things as the shortness of life and the longness of eternity.

He reported his avocation as: 'Being alive.'

He reported his principal occupation as: 'Being dead.'

THIS IS A CHRISTIAN NATION! ALL FOOT PLAY WILL BE PUNISHED BY THE HOOK said another sign. The sign was meaningless to me, since I had not yet learned Bokononists mingled their souls by pressing the bottoms of their feet together.

And the greatest mystery of all, since I had not read all of Philip Castle's book, was how Bokonon, bosom friend of Corporal McCabe, had come to be an outlaw.

## 62  Why Hazel Wasn't Scared

There were seven of us who got off at San Lorenzo: Newt and Angela, Ambassador Minton and his wife, H. Lowe Crosby and his wife, and I. When we had cleared customs, we were herded outdoors and on to a reviewing stand.

There, we faced a very quiet crowd.

Five thousand or more San Lorenzans stared at us. The islanders were oatmeal-coloured. The people were thin. There wasn't a fat person to be seen. Every person had teeth missing. Many legs were bowed or swollen.

Not one pair of eyes was clear.

The women's breasts were bare and paltry. The men wore loose loincloths that did little to conceal penes like pendulums on grandfather clocks.

There were many dogs, but not one barked. There were many infants, but not one cried. Here and there someone coughed – and that was all.

A military band stood at attention before the crowd. It did not play.

There was a colour guard before the band. It carried two banners, the Stars and Stripes and the flag of San Lorenzo. The flag of San Lorenzo consisted of a Marine Corporal's chevrons on a royal blue field. The banners hung lank in the windless day.

I imagined that somewhere far away I heard the blamming of a sledge on a brazen drum. There was no such sound. My soul was simply resonating the beat of the brassy, clanging heat of the San Lorenzan clime.

'I'm sure glad it's a Christian country,' Hazel Crosby whispered to her husband, 'or I'd be a little scared.'

Behind us was a xylophone.

There was a glittering sign on the xylophone. The sign was made of garnets and rhinestones.

The sign said MONA.

## 63 Reverent and Free

To the left side of our reviewing stand were six propeller-driven fighter planes in a row, military assistance from the United States to San Lorenzo. On the fuselage of each plane was painted, with childish bloodlust, a boa constrictor which was crushing a devil to death. Blood came from the devil's ears, nose, and mouth. A pitchfork was slipping from satanic red fingers.

Before each plane stood an oatmeal-coloured pilot; silent, too.

Then, above the tumid silence, there came a nagging song like the song of a gnat. It was a siren approaching. The siren was on 'Papa's' glossy black Cadillac limousine.

The limousine came to a stop before us, tyres smoking.

Out climbed 'Papa' Monzano, his adopted daughter, Mona Aamons Monzano, and Franklin Hoenikker.

At a limp, imperious signal from 'Papa', the crowd sang the San Lorenzan National Anthem. Its melody was 'Home on the Range'. The words had been written in 1922 by Lionel Boyd Johnson, by Bokonon. The words were these:

Oh, ours is a land
Where the living is grand,
And the men are as fearless as sharks;
The women are pure,
And we always are sure
That our children will all toe their marks.
San, San Lo-ren-zo!
What a rich, lucky island are we!
Our enemies quail,
For they know they will fail
Against people so reverent and free.

## 64  Peace and Plenty

And then the crowd was deathly still again.

'Papa' and Mona and Frank joined us on the reviewing stand. One snare drum played as they did so. The drumming stopped when 'Papa' pointed a finger at the drummer.

He wore a shoulder holster on the outside of his blouse. The weapon in it was a chromium-plated .45. He was an old, old man, as so many members of my *karass* were. He was in poor shape. His steps were small and bounceless. He was still a fat man, but his lard was melting fast, for his simple uniform was loose. The balls of his hoptoad eyes were yellow. His hands trembled.

His personal bodyguard was Major General Franklin Hoenikker, whose uniform was white. Frank – thin-wristed, narrow-shouldered – looked like a child kept up long after his customary bedtime. On his breast was a medal.

I observed the two, 'Papa' and Frank, with some difficulty – not because my view was blocked, but because I could not take my eyes off Mona. I was thrilled, heart-broken, hilarious, insane. Every greedy, unreasonable dream I'd ever had about what a woman should be came true in Mona. There, God love her warm and creamy soul, was peace and plenty forever.

That girl – and she was only eighteen – was rapturously serene. She seemed to understand all, and to be all there was to understand. In *The Books of Bokonon* she is mentioned by name. One thing Bokonon says of her is this: 'Mona has the simplicity of the all.'

Her dress was white and Greek.

She wore flat sandals on her small brown feet.

Her pale gold hair was lank and long.

Her hips were a lyre.

Oh God.

Peace and plenty forever.

She was the one beautiful girl in San Lorenzo. She was the national treasure. 'Papa' had adopted her, according to Philip Castle, in order to mingle divinity with the harshness of his rule.

The xylophone was rolled to the front of the stand. And Mona played it. She played 'When Day Is Done'. It was all tremolo – swelling, fading, swelling again.

The crowd was intoxicated by beauty.

And then it was time for 'Papa' to greet us.

## 65 *A Good Time to Come to San Lorenzo*

'Papa' was a self-educated man, who had been major-domo to Corporal McCabe. He had never been off the island. He spoke American English passably well.

Everything that any one of us said on the reviewing stand was bellowed out at the crowd through doomsday horns.

Whatever went out through those horns gabbled down a wide, short boulevard at the back of the crowd, ricocheted off the three glass-faced new buildings at the end of the boulevard, and came cackling back.

'Welcome,' said 'Papa'. 'You are coming to the best friend America ever had. America is misunderstood many places, but not here, Mr Ambassador.' He bowed to H. Lowe Crosby, the bicycle manufacturer, mistaking him for the new Ambassador.

'I know you've got a good country here, Mr President,' said Crosby. 'Everything I ever heard about it sounds great to me. There's just one thing . . .'

'Oh?'

'I'm not the Ambassador,' said Crosby. 'I wish I was, but I'm just a plain, ordinary businessman.' It hurt him to say who the real Ambassador was. 'This man over here is the big cheese.'

'Ah!' 'Papa' smiled at his mistake. The smile went away suddenly. Some pain inside of him made him wince, then made him hunch over, close his eyes – made him concentrate on surviving the pain.

Frank Hoenikker went to his support, feebly, incompetently. 'Are you all right?'

'Excuse me,' 'Papa' whispered at last, straightening up some. There were tears in his eyes. He brushed them away, straightening up all the way. 'I beg your pardon.'

He seemed to be in doubt for a moment as to where he was, as to what was expected of him. And then he remembered. He shook Horlick Minton's hand. 'Here, you are among friends.'

'I'm sure of it,' said Minton gently.

'Christian,' said 'Papa'.

'Good.'

'Anti-communists,' said 'Papa'.

'Good.'

'No communists here,' said 'Papa'. 'They fear the hook too much.'

'I should think they would,' said Minton.

'You have picked a very good time to come to us,' said 'Papa'. 'Tomorrow will be one of the happiest days in the history of our country. Tomorrow is our greatest national holiday, The Day of the Hundred Martyrs to Democracy. It will also be the day of the engagement of Major General Hoenikker to Mona Aamons Monzano, to the most precious person in my life and in the life of San Lorenzo.'

'I wish you much happiness, Miss Monzano,' said Minton warmly. 'And I congratulate *you*, General Hoenikker.'

The two young people nodded their thanks.

Minton now spoke of the so-called Hundred Martyrs to Democracy, and he told a whopping lie. 'There is not an American schoolchild who does not know the story of San Lorenzo's noble sacrifice in World War Two. The hundred brave San Lorenzans, whose day tomorrow is, gave as much as freedom-loving men can. The President of the United States has asked me to be his personal representative at ceremonies tomorrow, to cast a wreath, the gift of the American people to the people of San Lorenzo, on the sea.'

'The people of San Lorenzo thank you and your President and the generous people of the United States of America for their thoughtfulness,' said 'Papa'. 'We would be honoured if you would cast the wreath into the sea during the engagement party tomorrow.'

'The honour is mine.'

'Papa' commanded us all to honour him with our presence at the wreath ceremony and engagement party next day. We were to appear at his palace at noon.

'What children these two will have!' 'Papa' said, inviting us to stare at Frank and Mona. 'What blood! What beauty!'

The pain hit him again.

He again closed his eyes to huddle himself around that pain. He waited for it to pass, but it did not pass.

Still in agony, he turned away from us, faced the crowd and the microphone. He tried to gesture at the crowd, failed. He tried to say something to the crowd, failed.

And then the words came out. 'Go home,' he cried, strangling. 'Go home!'

The crowd scattered like leaves.

'Papa' faced us again, still grotesque in pain . . .

And then he collapsed.


## 66 *The Strongest Thing There Is*

He wasn't dead.

But he certainly looked dead; except that now and then, in the midst of all that seeming death, he would give a shivering twitch.

Frank protested loudly that 'Papa' wasn't dead, that he *couldn't* be dead. He was frantic. ' "Papa"! You can't die! You can't!'

Frank loosened 'Papa's' collar and blouse, rubbed his wrists. 'Give him air! Give "Papa" air!'

The fighter-plane pilots came running over to help us. One had sense enough to go for the airport ambulance.

The band and the colour guard, which had received no orders, remained at quivering attention.

I looked for Mona, found that she was still serene and had withdrawn to the rail of the reviewing stand. Death, if there was going to be death, did not alarm her.

Standing next to her was a pilot. He was not looking at her, but he had a perspiring radiance that I attributed to his being so near to her.

'Papa' now regained something like consciousness. With a hand that flapped like a captured bird, he pointed at Frank. 'You . . .' he said.

We all fell silent, in order to hear his words.

His lips moved, but we could hear nothing but bubbling sounds.

Somebody had what looked like a wonderful idea then – what looks like a hideous idea in retrospect. Someone – a pilot, I think – took the microphone from its mount and held it by 'Papa's' bubbling lips in order to amplify his words.

So death rattles and all sorts of spastic yodels bounced off the new buildings.

And then came words.

'You,' he said to Frank hoarsely, 'you – Franklin Hoenikker – you will be the next President of San Lorenzo. Science – you have science. Science is the strongest thing there is.

'Science,' said 'Papa'. 'Ice.' He rolled his yellow eyes, and he passed out again.

I looked at Mona.

Her expression was unchanged.

The pilot next to her, however, had his features composed in the catatonic, orgiastic rigidity of one receiving the Congressional Medal of Honour.

I looked down and I saw what I was not meant to see.

Mona had slipped off her sandal. Her small brown foot was bare.

And with that foot, she was kneading and kneading and kneading – obscenely kneading – the instep of the flyer's boot.

## 67 Hy-u-o-ook-kuh!

'Papa' didn't die – not then.

He was rolled away in the airport's big red meat wagon.

The Mintons were taken to their embassy by an American limousine.

Newt and Angela were taken to Frank's house in a San Lorenzan limousine.

The Crosbys and I were taken to the Casa Mona hotel in San Lorenzo's one taxi, a hearse-like 1939 Chrysler limousine with jump seats. The name on the side of the cab was Castle Transportation Inc. The cab was owned by Philip Castle, the owner of the Casa Mona, the son of the completely unselfish man I had come to interview.

The Crosbys and I were both upset. Our consternation was expressed in questions we had to have answered at once. The Crosbys wanted to know who Bokonon was. They were scandalized by the idea that anyone should be opposed to 'Papa' Monzano.

Irrelevantly, I found that I had to know at once who the Hundred Martyrs to Democracy had been.

The Crosbys got their answer first. They could not understand the San Lorenzan dialect, so I had to translate for them. Crosby's basic question to our driver was: 'Who the hell is this pissant Bokonon, anyway?'

'Very bad man,' said the driver. What he actually said was, *'Vorry ball moan.'*

'A communist?' asked Crosby, when he heard my translation.

'Oh, sure.'

'Has he got any following?'

'Sir?'

'Does anybody think he's any good?'

'Oh, no, sir,' said the driver piously. 'Nobody that crazy.'

'Why hasn't he been caught?' demanded Crosby.

'Hard man to find,' said the driver. 'Very smart.'

'Well, people must be hiding him and giving him food or he'd be caught by now.'

'Nobody hide him; nobody feed him. Everybody too smart to do that.'

'You sure?'

'Oh, sure,' said the driver. 'Anybody feed that crazy old man, anybody give him place to sleep, they get the hook. Nobody want the hook.'

He pronounced that last word: '*hy-u-o-ook-kuh*'.


## 68  Hoon-yera Mora-toorz

I asked the driver who the Hundred Martyrs to Democracy had been. The boulevard we were going down, I saw, was called the Boulevard of the Hundred Martyrs to Democracy.

The driver told me that San Lorenzo had declared war on Germany and Japan an hour after Pearl Harbor was attacked.

San Lorenzo conscripted a hundred men to fight on the side of democracy. These hundred men were put on a ship bound for the United States, where they were to be armed and trained.

The ship was sunk by a German submarine right outside of Bolivar harbour.

'*Dose, sore,*' he said, '*yeeara lo hoon-yera mora-toorz tut zamoo-cratz-ya.*'

'Those, sir,' he'd said in dialect, 'are the Hundred Martyrs to Democracy.'

## 69 A Big Mosaic

The Crosbys and I had the curious experience of being the very first guests of a new hotel. We were the first to sign the register of the Casa Mona.

The Crosbys got to the desk ahead of me, but H. Lowe Crosby was so startled by a wholly blank register that he couldn't bring himself to sign. He had to think about it a while.

'You sign,' he said to me. And then, defying me to think he was superstitious, he declared his wish to photograph a man who was making a huge mosaic on the fresh plaster of the lobby wall.

The mosaic was a portrait of Mona Aamons Monzano. It was twenty feet high. The man who was working on it was young and muscular. He sat at the top of a stepladder. He wore nothing but a pair of white duck trousers.

He was a white man.

The mosaicist was making the fine hairs on the nape of Mona's swan neck out of chips of gold.

Crosby went over to photograph him; came back to report that the man was the biggest pissant he had ever met. Crosby was the colour of tomato juice when he reported this. 'You can't say a damn thing to him that he won't turn inside out.'

So I went over to the mosaicist, watched him for a while, and then I told him, 'I envy you.'

'I always knew,' he sighed, 'that, if I waited long enough, somebody would come and envy me. I kept telling myself to be patient, that, sooner or later, somebody envious would come along.'

'Are you an American?'

'That happiness is mine.' He went right on working; he was incurious as to what I looked like. 'Do you want to take my photograph, too?'

'Do you mind?'

'I think, therefore I am, therefore I am photographable.'

'I'm afraid I don't have my camera with me.'

'Well, for Christ's sake, get it! You're not one of those people who trusts his memory, are you?'

'I don't think I'll forget that face you're working on very soon.'

'You'll forget it when you're dead, and so will I. When I'm dead, I'm going to forget everything – and I advise you to do the same.'

'Has she been posing for this or are you working from photographs or what?'

'I'm working from or what.'

'What?'

'I'm working from or what.' He tapped his temple. 'It's all in this enviable head of mine.'

'You know her?'

'That happiness is mine.'

'Frank Hoenikker's a lucky man.'

'Frank Hoenikker is a piece of shit.'

'You're certainly candid.'

'I'm also rich.'

'Glad to hear it.'

'If you want an expert opinion, money doesn't necessarily make people happy.'

'Thanks for the information. You've just saved me a lot of trouble. I was just about to make some money.'

'How?'

'Writing.'

'I wrote a book once.'

'What was it called?'

'*San Lorenzo,*' he said, '*the Land, the History, the People.*'


## 70  Tutored by Bokonon

'You, I take it,' I said to the mosaicist, 'are Philip Castle, son of Julian Castle.'

'That happiness is mine.'

'I'm here to see your father.'

'Are you an aspirin salesman?'

'No.'

'Too bad. Father's low on aspirin. How about miracle drugs? Father enjoys pulling off a miracle now and then.'

'I'm not a drug salesman. I'm a writer.'

'What makes you think a writer isn't a drug salesman?'

'I'll accept that. Guilty as charged.'

'Father needs some kind of book to read to people who are dying or in terrible pain. I don't suppose you've written anything like that.'

'Not yet.'

'I think there'd be money in it. There's another valuable tip for you.'

'I suppose I could overhaul the "Twenty-third Psalm", switch it around a little so nobody would realize it wasn't original with me.'

'Bokonon tried to overhaul it,' he told me. 'Bokonon found out he couldn't change a word.'

'You know him, too?'

'That happiness is mine. He was my tutor when I was a little boy.' He gestured sentimentally at the mosaic. 'He was Mona's tutor, too.'

'Was he a good teacher?'

'Mona and I can both read and write and do simple sums,' said Castle, 'if that's what you mean.'

## 71 *The Happiness of Being an American*

H. Lowe Crosby came over to have another go at Castle, the pissant.

'What do you call yourself,' sneered Crosby, 'a beatnik or what?'

'I call myself a Bokononist.'

'That's against the law in this country, isn't it?'

'I happen to have the happiness of being an American. I've been able to say I'm a Bokononist any time I damn please, and, so far, nobody's bothered me at all.'

'I believe in obeying the laws of whatever country I happen to be in.'

'You are not telling me the news.'

Crosby was livid. 'Screw you, Jack!'

'Screw you, Jasper,' said Castle mildly, 'and screw Mother's Day and Christmas, too.'

Crosby marched across the lobby to the desk clerk and he said, 'I want to report that man over there, that pissant, that so-called artist. You've got a nice little country here that's trying to attract the tourist trade and new investment in industry. The way that man talked to me, I don't ever want to see San Lorenzo again – and any friend who asks me about San Lorenzo, I'll tell him to keep the hell away. You may be getting a nice picture on the wall over there, but, by God, the pissant who's making it is the most insulting, discouraging son of a bitch I ever met in my life.'

The clerk looked sick. 'Sir . . .'

'I'm listening,' said Crosby, full of fire.

'Sir – he owns the hotel.'

## 72 *The Pissant Hilton*

H. Lowe Crosby and his wife checked out of the Casa Mona. Crosby called it 'The Pissant Hilton', and he demanded quarters at the American embassy.

So I was the only guest in a one-hundred-room hotel.

My room was a pleasant one. It faced, as did all the rooms, the Boulevard of the Hundred Martyrs to Democracy, Monzano Airport, and Bolivar harbour beyond. The Casa Mona was built like a bookcase, with solid sides and back and with a front of blue-green glass. The squalor and misery of the city, being to the sides and back of the Casa Mona, were impossible to see.

My room was air-conditioned. It was almost chilly. And, coming from the blamming heat into that chilliness, I sneezed.

There were fresh flowers on my bedside table, but my bed had not yet been made. There wasn't even a pillow on the bed. There was simply a bare, brand-new Beautyrest mattress. And there weren't any coat hangers in the closet; and there wasn't any toilet paper in the bathroom.

So I went out in the corridor to see if there was a chambermaid who would equip me a little more completely. There wasn't anybody out there, but there was a door open at the far end and very faint sounds of life.

I went to this door and found a large suite paved with drop-cloths. It was being painted, but the two painters weren't painting when I appeared. They were sitting on a shelf that ran the width of the window wall.

They had their shoes off. They had their eyes closed. They were facing each other.

They were pressing the soles of their bare feet together.

Each grasped his own ankles, giving himself the rigidity of a triangle.

I cleared my throat.

The two rolled off the shelf and fell to the spattered dropcloth. They landed on their hands and knees, and they stayed in that position – their behinds in the air, their noses close to the ground.

They were expecting to be killed.

'Excuse me,' I said, amazed.

'Don't tell,' begged one querulously. 'Please – please don't tell.'

'Tell what?'

'What you saw!'

'I didn't see anything.'

'If you tell,' he said, and he put his cheek to the floor and looked up at me beseechingly, 'if you tell, we'll die on the *hy-u-o-ook-kuh!*'

'Look, friends,' I said, 'either I came in too early or too late, but, I tell you again, I didn't see anything worth mentioning to anybody. Please – get up.'

They got up, their eyes still on me. They trembled and cowered. I convinced them at last that I would never tell what I had seen.

What I had seen, of course, was the Bokononist ritual of *boko-maru*, or the mingling of awarenesses.

We Bokononists believe that it is impossible to be sole-to-sole with another person without loving the person, provided the feet of both persons are clean and nicely tended.

The basis for the foot ceremony is this 'Calypso':

We will touch our feet, yes,
Yes, for all we're worth,
And we will love each other, yes,
Yes, like we love our Mother Earth.

## 73 *Black Death*

When I got back to my room I found that Philip Castle – mosaicist, historian, self-indexer, pissant, and hotel-keeper – was installing a roll of toilet paper in my bathroom.

'Thank you very much,' I said.

'You're entirely welcome.'

'This is what I'd call a hotel with a real heart. How many hotel owners would take such a direct interest in the comfort of a guest?'

'How many hotel owners have just one guest?'

'You used to have three.'

'Those were the days.'

'You know, I may be speaking out of turn, but I find it hard to understand how a person of your interests and talents would be attracted to the hotel business.'

He frowned perplexedly. 'I don't seem to be as good with guests as I might, do I?'

'I knew some people in the Hotel School at Cornell, and I can't help feeling they would have treated the Crosbys somewhat differently.'

He nodded uncomfortably. 'I know. I know.' He flapped his arms. 'Damned if I know why I built this hotel – something to do with my life, I guess. A way to be busy, a way not to be lonesome.' He shook his head. 'It was be a hermit or open a hotel – with nothing in between.'

'Weren't you raised at your father's hospital?'

'That's right. Mona and I both grew up there.'

'Well, aren't you at all tempted to do with your life what your father's done with his?'

Young Castle smiled wanly, avoiding a direct answer. 'He's a funny person, Father is,' he said. 'I think you'll like him.'

'I expect to. There aren't many people who've been as unselfish as he has.'

'One time,' said Castle, 'when I was about fifteen, there was a mutiny near here on a Greek ship bound from Hong Kong to Havana with a load of wicker furniture. The mutineers got control of the ship, didn't know how to run her, and smashed her up on the rocks near "Papa" Monzano's castle. Everybody drowned but the rats. The rats and the wicker furniture came ashore.'

That seemed to be the end of the story, but I couldn't be sure. 'So?'

'So some people got free furniture, and some people got bubonic plague. At Father's hospital, we had fourteen hundred deaths inside of ten days. Have you ever seen anyone die of bubonic plague?'

'That unhappiness has not been mine.'

'The lymph glands in the groin and the armpits swell to the size of grapefruit.'

'I can well believe it.'

'After death, the body turns black – coals to Newcastle in the case of San Lorenzo. When the plague was having everything its own way, the House of Hope and Mercy in the Jungle looked like Auschwitz or Buchenwald. We had stacks of dead so deep and wide that a bulldozer actually stalled trying to shove them towards a common grave. Father worked without sleep for days, worked not only without sleep but without saving many lives, either.'

Castle's grisly tale was interrupted by the ringing of my telephone.

'My God,' said Castle, 'I didn't even know the telephones were connected yet.'

I picked up the phone. 'Hello?'

It was Major General Franklin Hoenikker who had called me up. He sounded out of breath and scared stiff. 'Listen! You've got to come out to my house right away. We've got to have a talk! It could be a very important thing in your life!'

'Could you give me some idea?'

'Not on the phone, not on the phone. You come to my house. You come right away! Please!'

'All right.'

'I'm not kidding you. This is a really important thing in your life. This is the most important thing ever.' He hung up.

'What was that all about?' asked Castle.

'I haven't got the slightest idea. Frank Hoenikker wants to see me right away.'

'Take your time. Relax. He's a moron.'

'He said it was important.'

'How does he know what's important? I could carve a better man out of a banana.'

'Well, finish your story anyway.'

'Where was I?'

'The bubonic plague. The bulldozer was stalled by corpses.'

'Oh, yes. Anyway, one sleepless night I stayed up with Father while he worked. It was all we could do to find a live patient to treat. In bed after bed we found dead people.

'And Father started giggling,' Castle continued.

'He couldn't stop. He walked out into the night with his flashlight. He was still giggling. He was making the flashlight beam dance over all the dead people stacked outside. He put his hand on my head, and do you know what that marvellous man said to me?' asked Castle.

'Nope.'

'"Son," my father said to me, "someday this will all be yours."'

## 74 *Cat's Cradle*

I went to Frank's house in San Lorenzo's one taxicab.

We passed through scenes of hideous want. We climbed the slope of Mount McCabe. The air grew cooler. There was mist.

Frank's house had once been the home of Nestor Aamons, father of Mona, architect of the House of Hope and Mercy in the Jungle.

Aamons had designed it.

It straddled a waterfall; had a terrace cantilevered out into the mist rising from the fall. It was a cunning lattice of very light steel posts and beams. The interstices of the lattice were variously open, chinked with native stone, glazed, or curtained by sheets of canvas.

The effect of the house was not so much to enclose as to announce that a man had been whimsically busy there.

A servant greeted me politely and told me that Frank wasn't home yet. Frank was expected at any moment. Frank had left orders to the effect that I was to be made happy and comfortable, and that I was to stay for supper and the night. The servant, who introduced himself as Stanley, was the first plump San Lorenzan I had seen.

Stanley led me to my room; led me around the heart of the

house, down a staircase of living stone, a staircase sheltered or exposed by steel-framed rectangles at random. My bed was a foam-rubber slab on a stone shelf, a shelf of living stone. The walls of my chamber were canvas. Stanley demonstrated how I might roll them up or down, as I pleased.

I asked Stanley if anybody else was home, and he told me that only Newt was. Newt, he said, was out on the cantilevered terrace, painting a picture. Angela, he said, had gone sight-seeing to the House of Hope and Mercy in the Jungle.

I went out onto the giddy terrace that straddled the waterfall and found little Newt asleep in a yellow butterfly chair.

The painting on which Newt had been working was set on an easel next to the aluminium railing. The painting was framed in a misty view of sky, sea, and valley.

Newt's painting was small and black and warty.

It consisted of scratches made in a black, gummy impasto. The scratches formed a sort of spider's web, and I wondered if they might not be the sticky nets of human futility hung up on a moonless night to dry.

I did not wake up the midget who had made this dreadful thing. I smoked, listening to imagined voices in the water sounds.

What awakened little Newt was an explosion far away below. It caromed up the valley and went to God. It was a cannon on the water front of Bolivar, Frank's major-domo told me. It was fired every day at five.

Little Newt stirred.

While still half-snoozing, he put his black, painty hands to his mouth and chin, leaving black smears there. He rubbed his eyes and made black smears around them, too.

'Hello,' he said to me, sleepily.

'Hello,' I said. 'I like your painting.'

'You see what it is?'

'I suppose it means something different to everyone who sees it.'

'It's a cat's cradle.'

'Aha,' I said. 'Very good. The scratches are string. Right?'

'One of the oldest games there is, cat's cradle. Even the Eskimos know it.'

'You don't say.'

'For maybe a hundred thousand years or more, grownups have been waving tangles of string in their children's faces.'

'Um.'

Newt remained curled in the chair. He held out his painty hands as though a cat's cradle were strung between them. 'No wonder kids grow up crazy. A cat's cradle is nothing but a bunch of X's between somebody's hands, and little kids look and look and look at all those X's . . .'

'And?'

*'No damn cat, and no damn cradle.'*

## 75 Give My Regards to Albert Schweitzer

And then Angela Hoenikker Conners, Newt's beanpole sister, came in with Julian Castle, father of Philip, and founder of the House of Hope and Mercy in the Jungle. Castle wore a baggy white linen suit and a string tie. He had a scraggly moustache. He was bald. He was scrawny. He was a saint, I think.

He introduced himself to Newt and to me on the cantilevered terrace. He forestalled all reference to his possible saintliness by talking out of the corner of his mouth like a movie gangster.

'I understand you are a follower of Albert Schweitzer,' I said to him.

'At a distance . . .' He gave a criminal sneer. 'I've never met the gentleman.'

'He must surely know of your work, just as you know of his.'

'Maybe and maybe not. You ever see him?'

'No.'

'You ever expect to see him?'

'Someday maybe I will.'

'Well,' said Julian Castle, 'in case you run across Dr Schweitzer in your travels, you might tell him that he is *not* my hero.' He lit a big cigar.

When the cigar was going good and hot he pointed its red end at me. 'You can tell him he isn't my hero,' he said, 'but you can also tell him that, thanks to him, Jesus Christ *is*.'

'I think he'll be glad to hear it.'

'I don't give a damn if he is or not. This is something between Jesus and me.'


## 76 Julian Castle Agrees with Newt that Everything Is Meaningless

Julian Castle and Angela went to Newt's painting. Castle made a pinhole of a curled index finger, squinted at the painting through it.

'What do you think of it?' I asked him.

'It's *black*. What is it – hell?'

'It means whatever it means,' said Newt.

'Then it's hell,' snarled Castle.

'I was told a moment ago that it was a cat's cradle,' I said.

'Inside information always helps,' said Castle.

'I don't think it's very nice,' Angela complained. 'I think it's ugly, but I don't know anything about modern art. Sometimes I wish Newt would take some lessons, so he could know for sure if he was doing something or not.'

'Self-taught, are you?' Julian Castle asked Newt.

'Isn't everybody?' Newt inquired.

'Very good answer.' Castle was respectful.

I undertook to explain the deeper significance of the cat's cradle, since Newt seemed disinclined to go through that song and dance again.

And Castle nodded sagely. 'So this is a picture of the meaninglessness of it all! I couldn't agree more.'

'Do you *really* agree?' I asked. 'A minute ago you said something about Jesus.'

'Who?' said Castle.

'Jesus Christ?'

'Oh,' said Castle. '*Him.*' He shrugged. 'People have to talk about something just to keep their voice boxes in working order, so they'll have good voice boxes in case there's ever anything really meaningful to say.'

'I see.' I knew I wasn't going to have an easy time writing a popular article about him. I was going to have to concentrate on his saintly deeds and ignore entirely the satanic things he thought and said.

'You may quote me:' he said. 'Man is vile, and man makes nothing worth making, knows nothing worth knowing.'

He leaned down and he shook little Newt's painty hand. 'Right?'

Newt nodded, seeming to suspect momentarily that the case had been a little overstated. 'Right.'

And then the saint marched to Newt's painting and took it from its easel. He beamed at us all. 'Garbage – like everything else.'

And he threw the painting off the cantilevered terrace. It

sailed out on an updraught, stalled, boomeranged back, sliced into the waterfall.

There was nothing little Newt could say.

Angela spoke first. 'You've got paint all over your face, honey. Go wash it off.'

## 77 *Aspirin and* Boko-maru

'Tell me, Doctor,' I said to Julian Castle, 'how is "Papa" Monzano?'

'How would I know?'

'I thought you'd probably been treating him.'

'We don't speak . . .' Castle smiled. 'He doesn't speak to me, that is. The last thing he said to me, which was about three years ago, was that the only thing that kept me off the hook was my American citizenship.'

'What have you done to offend him? You come down here and with your own money found a free hospital for his people . . .'

' "Papa" doesn't like the way we treat the whole patient,' said Castle, 'particularly the whole patient when he's dying. At the House of Hope and Mercy in the Jungle, we administer the last rites of the Bokononist Church to those who want them.'

'What are the rites like?'

'Very simple. They start with a responsive reading. You want to respond?'

'I'm not that close to death just now, if you don't mind.'

He gave me a grisly wink. 'You're wise to be cautious. People taking the last rites have a way of dying on cue. I think we could keep you from going all the way, though, if we didn't touch feet.'

'Feet?'

He told me about the Bokononist attitude relative to feet.

'That explains something I saw in the hotel.' I told him about the two painters on the window sill.

'It works, you know,' he said. 'People who do that really do feel better about each other and the world.'

'Um.'

'*Boko-maru*.'

'Sir?'

'That's what the foot business is called,' said Castle. 'It works. I'm grateful for things that work. Not many things *do* work, you know.'

'I suppose not.'

'I couldn't possibly run that hospital of mine if it weren't for aspirin and *boko-maru*.'

'I gather,' I said, 'that there are still several Bokononists on the island, despite the laws, despite the *hy-u-o-ook-kuh* . . .'

He laughed. 'You haven't caught on, yet?'

'To what?'

'Everybody on San Lorenzo is a devout Bokononist, the *hy-u-o-ook-kuh* notwithstanding.'

## 78 Ring of Steel

'When Bokonon and McCabe took over this miserable country years ago,' said Julian Castle, 'they threw out the priests. And then Bokonon, cynically and playfully, invented a new religion.'

'I know.' I said.

'Well, when it became evident that no governmental or economic reform was going to make the people much less miserable, the religion became the one real instrument of hope. Truth was the enemy of the people, because the truth was so terrible, so Bokonon made it his business to provide the people with better and better lies.'

'How did he come to be an outlaw?'

'It was his own idea. He asked McCabe to outlaw him and his religion, too, in order to give the religious life of the people more zest, more tang. He wrote a little poem about it, incidentally.'

Castle quoted this poem, which does not appear in *The Books of Bokonon*:

> So I said good-bye to government,
> And I gave my reason:
> That a really good religion
> Is a form of treason.

'Bokonon suggested the hook, too, as the proper punishment for Bokononists,' he said. 'It was something he'd seen in the Chamber of Horrors at Madame Tussaud's.' He winked ghoulishly. 'That was for zest, too.'

'Did many people die on the hook?'

'Not at first, not at first. At first it was all make-believe. Rumours were cunningly circulated about executions, but no one really knew anyone who had died that way. McCabe had a good old time making bloodthirsty threats against the Bokononists – which was everybody.

'And Bokonon went into cosy hiding in the jungle,' Castle continued, 'where he wrote and preached all day long and ate good things his disciples brought him.

'McCabe would organize the unemployed, which was practically everybody, into great Bokonon hunts.

'About every six months McCabe would announce

triumphantly that Bokonon was surrounded by a ring of steel, which was remorselessly closing in.

'And then the leaders of the remorseless ring would have to report to McCabe, full of chagrin and apoplexy, that Bokonon had done the impossible.

'He had escaped, had evaporated, had lived to preach another day. Miracle!'

## 79  Why McCabe's Soul Grew Coarse

'McCabe and Bokonon did not succeed in raising what is generally thought of as the standard of living,' said Castle. 'The truth was that life was as short and brutish and mean as ever.

'But people didn't have to pay as much attention to the awful truth. As the living legend of the cruel tyrant in the city and the gentle holy man in the jungle grew, so, too, did the happiness of the people grow. They were all employed full time as actors in a play they understood, that any human being anywhere could understand and applaud.'

'So life became a work of art,' I marvelled.

'Yes. There was only one trouble with it.'

'Oh?'

'The drama was very tough on the souls of the two main actors, McCabe and Bokonon. As young men, they had been pretty much alike, had both been half-angel, half-pirate.

'But the drama demanded that the pirate half of Bokonon and the angel half of McCabe wither away. And McCabe and Bokonon paid a terrible price in agony for the happiness of the people – McCabe knowing the agony of the tyrant and Bokonon knowing the agony of the saint. They both became, for all practical purposes, insane.'

Castle crooked the index finger of his left hand. 'And then, people really did start dying on the *hy-u-o-ook-kuh*.'

'But Bokonon was never caught?' I asked.

'McCabe never went that crazy. He never made a really serious effort to catch Bokonon. It would have been easy to do.'

'Why didn't he catch him?'

'McCabe was always sane enough to realize that without the holy man to war against, he himself would become meaningless. "Papa" Monzano understands that, too.'

'Do people still die on the hook?'

'It's inevitably fatal.'

'I mean,' I said, 'does "Papa" really have people executed that way?'

'He executes one every two years – just to keep the pot boiling, so to speak.' He sighed, looking up at the evening sky. 'Busy, busy, busy.'

'Sir?'

'It's what we Bokononists say,' he said, 'when we feel that a lot of mysterious things are going on.'

'You?' I was amazed. 'A Bokononist, too?'

He gazed at me levelly. 'You, too. You'll find out.'

## 80 *The Waterfall Strainers*

Angela and Newt were on the cantilevered terrace with Julian Castle and me. We had cocktails. There was still no word from Frank.

Both Angela and Newt, it appeared, were fairly heavy drinkers. Castle told me that his days as a playboy had cost him a kidney, and that he was unhappily compelled, perforce, to stick to ginger ale.

Angela, when she got a few drinks into her, complained of how the world had swindled her father. 'He gave so much, and they gave him so little.'

I pressed her for examples of the world's stinginess and got some exact numbers. 'General Forge and Foundry gave him a forty-five-dollar bonus for every patent his work led to,' she said. 'That's the same patent bonus they paid anybody in the company.' She shook her head mournfully. 'Forty-five dollars – and just think what some of those patents were for!'

'Um,' I said. 'I assume he got a salary, too.'

'The most he ever made was twenty-eight thousand dollars a year.'

'I'd say that was pretty good.'

She got very huffy. 'You know what movie stars make?'

'A lot, sometimes.'

'You know Dr Breed made ten thousand more dollars a year than Father did?'

'That was certainly an injustice.'

'I'm sick of injustice.'

She was so shrilly exercised that I changed the subject. I asked Julian Castle what he thought had become of the painting he had thrown down the waterfall.

'There's a little village at the bottom,' he told me. 'Five or ten shacks, I'd say. It's "Papa" Monzano's birthplace, incidentally. The waterfall ends in a big stone bowl there.

'The villagers have a net made of chicken wire stretched across a notch in the bowl. Water spills out through the notch into a stream.'

'And Newt's painting is in the net now, you think?' I asked.

'This is a poor country – in case you haven't noticed,' said Castle. 'Nothing stays in the net very long. I imagine Newt's painting is being dried in the sun by now, along with the butt of my cigar. Four square feet of gummy canvas, the four milled and mitred sticks of the stretcher, some tacks, too, and a cigar. All in all, a pretty nice catch for some poor, poor man.'

'I could just scream sometimes,' said Angela, 'when I think about how much some people get paid and how little they paid Father – and how much he gave.' She was on the edge of a crying jag.

'Don't cry,' Newt begged her gently.

'Sometimes I can't help it,' she said.

'Go get your clarinet,' urged Newt. 'That always helps.'

I thought at first that this was a fairly comical suggestion. But then, from Angela's reaction, I learned that the suggestion was serious and practical.

'When I get this way,' she said to Castle and me, 'sometimes it's the only thing that helps.'

But she was too shy to get her clarinet right away. We had to keep begging her to play, and she had to have two more drinks.

'She's really just wonderful,' little Newt promised.

'I'd love to hear you play,' said Castle.

'All right,' said Angela finally as she rose unsteadily. 'All right – I will.'

When she was out of earshot, Newt apologized for her. 'She's had a tough time. She needs a rest.'

'She's been sick?' I asked.

'Her husband is mean as hell to her,' said Newt. He showed us that he hated Angela's handsome young husband, the extremely successful Harrison C. Conners, President of Fabri-Tek. 'He hardly ever comes home – and, when he does, he's drunk and generally covered with lipstick.'

'From the way she talked,' I said, 'I thought it was a very happy marriage.'

Little Newt held his hands six inches apart and he spread his fingers. 'See the cat? See the cradle?'

## 81 *A White Bride for the Son of a Pullman Porter*

I did not know what was going to come from Angela's clarinet. No one could have imagined what was going to come from there.

I expected something pathological, but I did not expect the depth, the violence, and the almost intolerable beauty of the disease.

Angela moistened and warmed the mouthpiece, but did not blow a single preliminary note. Her eyes glazed over, and her long, bony fingers twittered idly over the noiseless keys.

I waited anxiously, and I remembered what Marvin Breed had told me – that Angela's one escape from her bleak life with her father was to her room, where she would lock the door and play along with phonograph records.

Newt now put a long-playing record on the large phonograph in the room off the terrace. He came back with the record's slipcase, which he handed to me.

The record was called *Cat House Piano*. It was of unaccompanied piano music by Meade Lux Lewis.

Since Angela, in order to deepen her trance, let Lewis play his first number without joining him, I read some of what the jacket said about Lewis.

'Born in Louisville, Ky., in 1905,' I read, 'Mr Lewis didn't turn to music until he had passed his 16th birthday and then the instrument provided by his father was the violin. A year later young Lewis chanced to hear Jimmy Yancey play the piano. "This," as Lewis recalls, "was the real thing." Soon,' I read, 'Lewis was teaching himself to play the boogie-woogie piano, absorbing all that was possible from the older Yancey, who remained until his death a close friend and idol to Mr Lewis. Since his father was a Pullman porter,' I read, 'the Lewis family lived near the railroad. The rhythm of the trains soon became a natural pattern to young Lewis and he composed the boogie-woogie solo, now a classic of its kind, which became known as "Honky Tonk Train Blues".'

I looked up from my reading. The first number on the record was done. The phonograph needle was now scratching its slow way across the void to the second. The second number, I learned from the jacket, was 'Dragon Blues'.

Meade Lux Lewis played four bars alone – and then Angela Hoenikker joined in.

Her eyes were closed.

I was flabbergasted.

She was great.

She improvised around the music of the Pullman porter's son; went from liquid lyricism to rasping lechery to the shrill skittishness of a frightened child, to a heroin nightmare.

Her glissandi spoke of heaven and hell and all that lay between.

Such music from such a woman could only be a case of schizophrenia or demonic possession.

My hair stood on end, as though Angela were rolling on the floor, foaming at the mouth, and babbling fluent Babylonian.

When the music was done, I shrieked at Julian Castle, who was transfixed, too, 'My God – life! Who can understand even one little minute of it?'

'Don't try,' he said. 'Just pretend you understand.'

'That's – that's very good advice.' I went limp.

Castle quoted another poem:

> Tiger got to hunt,
> Bird got to fly;
> Man got to sit and wonder, 'Why, why, why?'
> Tiger got to sleep,
> Bird got to land;
> Man got to tell himself he understand.

'What's that from?' I asked.

'What could it possibly be from but *The Books of Bokonon*?'

'I'd love to see a copy sometime.'

'Copies are hard to come by,' said Castle. 'They aren't printed. They're made by hand. And, of course, there is no such thing as a completed copy, since Bokonon is adding things every day.'

Little Newt snorted. 'Religion!'

'Beg your pardon?' Castle said.

'See the cat?' asked Newt. 'See the cradle?'

## 82 Zah-mah-ki-bo

Major General Franklin Hoenikker didn't appear for supper.

He telephoned, and insisted on talking to me and to no one else. He told me that he was keeping a vigil by 'Papa's' bed; that 'Papa' was dying in great pain. Frank sounded scared and lonely.

'Look,' I said, 'why don't I go back to my hotel, and you and I can get together later, when this crisis is over?'

'No, no, no. You stay right there! I want you to be where I can get hold of you right away!' He was panicky about my slipping out of his grasp. Since I couldn't account for his interest in me, I began to feel panic, too.

'Could you give me some idea what you want to see me about?' I asked.

'Not over the telephone.'

'Something about your father?'

'Something about *you*.'

'Something I've done?'

'Something you're *going* to do.'

I heard a chicken clucking in the background of Frank's end of the line. I heard a door open, and xylophone music came from some chamber. The music was again 'When Day Is Done'. And then the door was closed, and I couldn't hear the music any more.

'I'd appreciate it if you'd give me some small hint of what you expect me to do – so I can sort of get set,' I said.

'*Zah-mah-ki-bo*.'

'What?'

'It's a Bokononist word.'

'I don't know any Bokononist words.'

'Julian Castle's there?'

'Yes.'

'Ask him,' said Frank. 'I've got to go now.' He hung up.

So I asked Julian Castle what *zah-mah-ki-bo* meant.

'You want a simple answer or a whole answer?'

'Let's start with a simple one.'

'Fate – inevitable destiny.'

## 83 *Dr Schlichter von Koenigswald Approaches the Break-even Point*

'Cancer,' said Julian Castle at dinner, when I told him that 'Papa' was dying in pain.

'Cancer of what?'

'Cancer of about everything. You say he collapsed on the reviewing stand today?'

'He sure did,' said Angela.

'That was the effect of drugs,' Castle declared. 'He's at the point now where drugs and pain just about balance out. More drugs would kill him.'

'I'd kill myself, I think,' murmured Newt. He was sitting on a sort of folding high chair he took with him when he went visiting. It was made of aluminium tubing and canvas. 'It beats sitting on a dictionary, an atlas, and a telephone book,' he'd said when he erected it.

'That's what Corporal McCabe did, of course,' said Castle. 'He named his major-domo as his successor, then he shot himself.'

'Cancer, too?' I asked.

'I can't be sure; I don't think so, though. Unrelieved villainy just wore him out, is my guess. That was all before my time.'

'This is certainly a cheerful conversation,' said Angela.

'I think everybody would agree that these are cheerful times,' said Castle.

'Well,' I said to him, 'I'd think you would have more reasons for being cheerful than most, doing what you are doing with your life.'

'I once had a yacht, too, you know.'

'I don't follow you.'

'Having a yacht is a reason for being more cheerful than most, too.'

'If you aren't "Papa's" doctor,' I said, 'who is?'

'One of my staff, a Dr Schlichter von Koenigswald.'

'A German?'

'Vaguely. He was in the S.S. for fourteen years. He was a camp physician at Auschwitz for six of those years.'

'Doing penance at the House of Hope and Mercy, is he?'

'Yes,' said Castle, 'and making great strides, too, saving lives right and left.'

'Good for him.'

'Yes. If he keeps going at his present rate, working night and day, the number of people he's saved will equal the number of people he let die – in the year 3010.'

So there's another member of my *karass*: Dr Schlichter von Koenigswald.

## 84 Blackout

Three hours after supper Frank still hadn't come home. Julian Castle excused himself and went back to the House of Hope and Mercy in the Jungle.

Angela and Newt and I sat on the cantilevered terrace. The lights of Bolivar were lovely below us. There was a great illuminated cross on top of the administration building of Monzano Airport. It was motor-driven, turning slowly, boxing the compass with electric piety.

There were other bright places on the island, too, to the north of us. Mountains prevented our seeing them directly, but we could see in the sky their balloons of light. I asked Stanley,

Frank Hoenikker's major-domo, to identify for me the sources of the auroras.

He pointed them out, counter-clockwise. 'House of Hope and Mercy in the Jungle, "Papa's" palace, and Fort Jesus.'

'Fort Jesus?'

'The training camp for our soldiers.'

'It's named after Jesus Christ?'

'Sure. Why not?'

There was a new balloon of light growing quickly to the north. Before I could ask what it was, it revealed itself as headlights topping a ridge. The headlights were coming towards us. They belonged to a convoy.

The convoy was composed of five American-made army trucks. Machine gunners manned ring mounts on the tops of the cabs.

The convoy stopped in Frank's driveway. Soldiers dismounted at once. They set to work on the grounds, digging foxholes and machine-gun pits. I went out with Frank's major-domo to ask the officer in charge what was going on.

'We have been ordered to protect the next President of San Lorenzo,' said the officer in island dialect.

'He isn't here now,' I informed him.

'I don't know anything about it,' he said. 'My orders are to dig in here. That's all I know.'

I told Angela and Newt about it.

'Do you think there's any real danger?' Angela asked me.

'I'm a stranger here myself,' I said.

At that moment there was a power failure. Every electric light in San Lorenzo went out.

## 85  *A Pack of* Foma

Frank's servants brought us gasoline lanterns; told us that power failures were common in San Lorenzo, that there was no cause for alarm. I found that disquiet was hard for me to set aside, however, since Frank had spoken of my *zah-mah-ki-bo*.

He had made me feel as though my own free will were as irrelevant as the free will of a piggy-wig arriving at the Chicago stockyards.

I remembered again the stone angel in Ilium.

And I listened to the soldiers outside – to their clinking, chunking, murmuring labours.

I was unable to concentrate on the conversation of Angela and Newt, though they got onto a fairly interesting subject. They told me that their father had had an identical twin. They had never met him. His name was Rudolph. The last they had heard of him, he was a music-box manufacturer in Zurich, Switzerland.

'Father hardly ever mentioned him,' said Angela.

'Father hardly ever mentioned anybody,' Newt declared.

There was a sister of the old man, too, they told me. Her name was Celia. She raised giant schnauzers on Shelter Island, New York.

'She always sends a Christmas card,' said Angela.

'With a picture of a giant schnauzer on it,' said little Newt.

'It sure is funny how different people in different families turn out,' Angela observed.

'That's very true and well said,' I agreed. I excused myself from the glittering company, and asked Stanley, the major-domo, if there happened to be a copy of *The Books of Bokonon* about the house.

Stanley pretended not to know what I was talking about.

And then he grumbled that *The Books of Bokonon* were filth. And then he insisted that anyone who read them should die on the hook. And then he brought me a copy from Frank's bedside table.

It was a heavy thing, about the size of an unabridged dictionary. It was written by hand. I trundled it off to my bedroom, to my slab of rubber on living rock.

There was no index, so my search for the implications of *zah-mah-ki-bo* was difficult; was, in fact, fruitless that night.

I learned some things, but they were scarcely helpful. I learned of the Bokononist cosmogony, for instance, wherein *Borasisi*, the sun, held *Pabu*, the moon, in his arms, and hoped that *Pabu* would bear him a fiery child.

But poor *Pabu* gave birth to children that were cold, that did not burn; and *Borasisi* threw them away in disgust. These were the planets, who circled their terrible father at a safe distance.

Then poor *Pabu* herself was cast away, and she went to live with her favourite child, which was Earth. Earth was *Pabu*'s favourite because it had people on it; and the people looked up at her and loved her and sympathized.

And what opinion did Bokonon hold of his own cosmogony? '*Foma!* Lies!' he wrote. 'A pack of *foma!*'

## 86 *Two Little Jugs*

It's hard to believe that I slept at all, but I must have – for, otherwise, how could I have found myself awakened by a series of bangs and a flood of light?

I rolled out of bed at the first bang and ran to the heart of the house in the brainless ecstasy of a volunteer fireman.

I found myself rushing headlong at Newt and Angela, who were fleeing from beds of their own.

We all stopped short, sheepishly analysing the nightmarish sounds around us, sorting them out as coming from a radio, from an electric dishwasher, from a pump – all restored to noisy life by the return of electric power.

The three of us awakened enough to realize that there was humour in our situation, that we had reacted in amusingly human ways to a situation that seemed mortal but wasn't. And, to demonstrate my mastery over my illusory fate, I turned the radio off.

We all chuckled.

And we all vied, in saving face, to be the greatest student of human nature, the person with the quickest sense of humour.

Newt was the quickest; he pointed out to me that I had my passport and my billfold and my wristwatch in my hands. I had no idea what I'd grabbed in the face of death – didn't know I'd grabbed anything.

I countered hilariously by asking Angela and Newt why it was that they both carried little Thermos jugs, identical red-and-grey jugs capable of holding about three cups of coffee.

It was news to them both that they were carrying such jugs. They were shocked to find them in their hands.

They were spared making an explanation by more banging outside. I was bound to find out what the banging was right away; and, with a brazenness as unjustified as my earlier panic, I investigated, found Frank Hoenikker outside tinkering with a motor-generator set mounted on a truck.

The generator was the new source of our electricity. The gasoline motor that drove it was backfiring and smoking. Frank was trying to fix it.

He had the heavenly Mona with him. She was watching him as always, gravely.

'Boy, have I got news for you!' he yelled at me, and he led the way back into the house.

Angela and Newt were still in the living room, but, somehow, somewhere, they managed to get rid of their peculiar Thermos jugs.

The contents of those jugs, of course, were parts of the legacies from Dr Felix Hoenikker, were parts of the *wampeter* of my *karass*, were chips of *ice-nine*.

Frank took me aside. 'How awake are you?'

'As awake as I ever was.'

'I hope you're really wide awake, because we've got to have a talk right now.'

'Start talking.'

'Let's get some privacy.' Frank told Mona to make herself comfortable. 'We'll call you if we need you.'

I looked at Mona, meltingly, and I thought that I had never needed anyone as much as I needed her.


## 87 *The Cut of My Jib*

About this Franklin Hoenikker – the pinch-faced child spoke with the timbre and conviction of a kazoo. I had heard it said in the Army that such and such a man spoke like a man with a paper rectum. Such a man was General Hoenikker. Poor Frank had had almost no experience in talking to anyone, having spent a furtive childhood as Secret Agent X-9.

Now, hoping to be hearty and persuasive, he said tinny things to me, things like, 'I like the cut of your jib!' and 'I want to talk cold turkey to you, man to man!'

And he took me down to what he called his 'den' in order that we might, '. . . call a spade a spade, and let the chips fall where they may.'

So we went down steps cut into a cliff and into a natural cave that was beneath and behind the waterfall. There were a couple of drawing tables down there; three pale, bare-boned Scandinavian chairs; a bookcase containing books on architecture, books in German, French, Finnish, Italian, English.

All was lit by electric lights, lights that pulsed with the panting of the motor-generator set.

And the most striking thing about the cave was that there were pictures painted on the walls, painted with kindergarten boldness, painted with the flat clay, earth, and charcoal colours of very early man. I did not have to ask Frank how old the cave paintings were. I was able to date them by their subject. The paintings were not of mammoths or sabre-toothed tigers or ithyphallic cave bears.

The paintings treated endlessly the aspects of Mona Aamons Monzano as a little girl.

'This – this is where Mona's father worked?' I asked.

'That's right. He was the Finn who designed the House of Hope and Mercy in the Jungle.'

'I know.'

'That isn't what I brought you down here to talk about.'

'This is something about your father?'

'This is about *you*.' Frank put his hand on my shoulder and he looked me in the eye. The effect was dismaying. Frank meant to inspire camaraderie, but his head looked to me like a bizarre little owl, blinded by light and perched on a tall white post.

'Maybe you'd better come to the point.'

'There's no sense in beating around the bush,' he said. 'I'm a pretty good judge of character, if I do say so myself, and I like the cut of your jib.'

'Thank you.'

'I think you and I could really hit it off.'

'I have no doubt of it.'

'We've both got things that mesh.'

I was grateful when he took his hand from my shoulder. He meshed the fingers of his hands like gear teeth. One hand represented him, I suppose, and the other represented me.

'We need each other.' He wiggled his fingers to show me how gears worked.

I was silent for some time, though outwardly friendly.

'Do you get my meaning?' asked Frank at last.

'You and I – we're going to *do* something together?'

'That's right!' Frank clapped his hands. 'You're a worldly person, used to meeting the public; and I'm a technical person, used to working behind the scenes, making things go.'

'How can you possibly know what kind of a person I am? We've just met.'

'Your clothes, the way you talk.' He put his hand on my shoulder again. 'I like the cut of your jib!'

'So you said.'

Frank was frantic for me to complete his thought, to do it enthusiastically, but I was still at sea. 'Am I to understand that . . . that you are offering me some kind of job here, here in San Lorenzo?'

He clapped his hands. He was delighted. 'That's right! What would you say to a hundred thousand dollars a year?'

'Good God!' I cried. 'What would I have to do for that?'

'Practically nothing. And you'd drink out of gold goblets every night and eat off of gold plates and have a palace all your own.'

'What's the job?'

'President of the Republic of San Lorenzo.'

## 88  *Why Frank Couldn't Be President*

'Me? President?' I gasped.

'Who else is there?'

'Nuts!'

'Don't say no until you've really thought about it.' Frank watched me anxiously.

'No!'

'You haven't really thought about it.'

'Enough to know it's crazy.'

Frank made his fingers into gears again. 'We'd work *together*. I'd be backing you up all the time.'

'Good. So, if I got plugged from the front you'd get it, too.'

'Plugged?'

'Shot! Assassinated!'

Frank was mystified. 'Why would anybody shoot you?'

'So he could get to be President.'

Frank shook his head. 'Nobody in San Lorenzo *wants* to be President,' he promised me. 'It's against their religion.'

'It's against *your* religion, too? I thought *you* were going to be the next President.'

'I . . .' he said, and found it hard to go on. He looked haunted.

'You what?' I asked.

He faced the sheet of water that curtained the cave. 'Maturity, the way I understand it,' he told me, 'is knowing what your limitations are.'

He wasn't far from Bokonon in defining maturity. 'Maturity,' Bokonon tells us, 'is a bitter disappointment for which no remedy exists, unless laughter can be said to remedy anything.'

'I know I've got limitations,' Frank continued. 'They're the same limitations my father had.'

'Oh?'

'I've got a lot of very good ideas, just the way my father had,' Frank told me and the waterfall, 'but he was no good at facing the public, and neither am I.'

## 89 Duffle

'You'll take the job?' Frank inquired anxiously.

'No,' I told him.

'Do you know anybody who *might* want the job?' Frank was giving a classic illustration of what Bokonon calls *duffle. Duffle*, in the Bokononist sense, is the destiny of thousands upon thousands of persons when placed in the hands of a *stuppa*. A *stuppa* is a fogbound child.

I laughed.

'Something's funny?'

'Pay no attention when I laugh,' I begged him. 'I'm a notorious pervert in that respect.'

'Are you laughing at me?'

I shook my head. 'No.'

'Word of honour?'

'Word of honour.'

'People used to make fun of me all the time.'

'You must have imagined that.'

'They used to yell things at me. I didn't imagine *that*.'

'People are unkind sometimes without meaning to be,' I suggested. I wouldn't have given him my word of honour on that.

'You know what they used to yell at me?'

'No.'

'They used to yell at me, "Hey, X-9, where you going?"'

'That doesn't seem too bad.'

'That's what they used to call me,' said Frank in sulky reminiscence, '"Secret Agent X-9."'

I didn't tell him I knew that already.

'"Where are you going, X-9?"' Frank echoed again.

I imagined what the taunters had been like, imagined where Fate had eventually goosed and chivvied them to. The wits who had yelled at Frank were surely nicely settled in death-like jobs at General Forge and Foundry, at Ilium Power and Light, at the Telephone Company . . .

And here, by God, was Secret Agent X-9, a Major General, offering to make me king . . . in a cave that was curtained by a tropical waterfall.

'They really would have been surprised if I'd stopped and told them where I was going.'

'You mean you had some premonition you'd end up here?' It was a Bokononist question.

'I was going to Jack's Hobby Shop,' he said, with no sense of anticlimax.

'Oh.'

'They all knew I was going there, but they didn't know what really went on there. They would have been really surprised – especially the girls – if they'd found out what *really* went on. The girls didn't think I knew anything about girls.'

'What *really* went on?'

'I was screwing Jack's wife every day. That's how come I fell asleep all the time in high school. That's how come I never achieved my full potential.'

He roused himself from this sordid recollection. 'Come on. Be President of San Lorenzo. You'd be real good at it, with your personality. Please?'

## 90 Only One Catch

And the time of night and the cave and the waterfall – and the stone angel in Ilium . . .

And 250,000 cigarettes and 3,000 quarts of booze, and two wives and no wife . . .

And no love waiting for me anywhere . . .

And the listless life of an ink-stained hack . . .

And *Pabu*, the moon, and *Borasisi*, the sun, and their children . . .

All things conspired to form one cosmic *vin-dit*, one mighty shove into Bokononism, into the belief that God was running my life and that He had work for me to do.

And, inwardly, I *sarooned*, which is to say that I acquiesced to the seeming demands of my *vin-dit*.

Inwardly, I agreed to become the next President of San Lorenzo.

Outwardly, I was still guarded, suspicious. 'There must be a catch,' I hedged.

'There isn't.'

'There'll be an election?'

'There never has been. We'll just announce who the new President is.'

'And nobody will object?'

'Nobody objects to anything. They aren't interested. They don't care.'

'There *has* to be a catch!'

'There's kind of one,' Frank admitted.

'I knew it!' I began to shrink from my *vin-dit*. 'What is it? What's the catch?'

'Well, it isn't really a catch, because you don't have to do it, if you don't want to. It *would* be a good idea, though.'

'Let's hear this great idea.'

'Well, if you're going to be President, I think you really ought to marry Mona. But you don't have to, if you don't want to. You're the boss.'

'She would *have* me?'

'If she'd have me, she'd have you. All you have to do is ask her.'

'Why should she say yes?'

'It's predicted in *The Books of Bokonon* that she'll marry the next President of San Lorenzo,' said Frank.

## 91 Mona

Frank brought Mona to her father's cave and left us alone.

We had difficulty in speaking at first. I was shy.

Her gown was diaphanous. Her gown was azure. It was a simple gown, caught lightly at the waist by a gossamer thread. All else was shaped by Mona herself. Her breasts were like pomegranates or what you will, but like nothing so much as a young woman's breasts.

Her feet were all but bare. Her toenails were exquisitely manicured. Her scanty sandals were gold.

'How – how do you do?' I asked. My heart was pounding. Blood boiled in my ears.

'It is not possible to make a mistake,' she assured me.

I did not know that this was a customary greeting given by all Bokononists when meeting a shy person. So, I responded with a feverish discussion of whether it was possible to make a mistake or not.

'My God, you have no idea how many mistakes I've already made. You're looking at the world's champion mistake maker,'

I blurted – and so on. 'Do you have any idea what Frank just said to me?'

'About *me?*'

'About everything, but *especially* about you.'

'He told you that you could have me, if you wanted.'

'Yes.'

'That's true.'

'I – I – I . . .'

'Yes?'

'I don't know what to say next.'

'*Boko-maru* would help,' she suggested.

'What?'

'Take off your shoes,' she commanded. And she removed her sandals with the utmost grace.

I am a man of the world, having had, by a reckoning I once made, more than fifty-three women. I can say that I have seen women undress themselves in every way that it can be done. I have watched the curtains part on every variation of the final act.

And yet, the one woman who made me groan involuntarily did no more than remove her sandals.

I tried to untie my shoes. No bridegroom ever did worse. I got one shoe off, but knotted the other one tight. I tore a thumbnail on the knot; finally ripped off the shoe without untying it.

Then off came my socks.

Mona was already sitting on the floor, her legs extended, her round arms thrust behind her for support, her head tilted back, her eyes closed.

It was up to me now to complete my first – my first – my first, Great God . . .

*Boko-maru.*

## 92 *On the Poet's Celebration of His First* Boko-maru

These are not Bokonon's words. They are mine.

> Sweet wraith,
> Invisible mist of . . .
> I am –
> My soul –
> Wraith lovesick o'erlong,
> O'erlong alone:
> Wouldst another sweet soul meet?
> Long have I
> Advised thee ill
> As to where two souls
> Might tryst.
> My soles, my soles!
> My soul, my soul,
> Go there,
> Sweet soul;
> Be kissed.
> Mmmmmmm.

## 93 *How I Almost Lost My Mona*

'Do you find it easier to talk to me now?' Mona inquired.

'As though I'd known you for a thousand years,' I confessed. I felt like crying. 'I love you, Mona.'

'I love you.' She said it simply.

'What a fool Frank was!'

'Oh?'

'To give you up.'

'He did not love me. He was going to marry me only because "Papa" wanted him to. He loves another.'

'Who?'

'A woman he knew in Ilium.'

The lucky woman had to be the wife of the owner of Jack's Hobby Shop. 'He told you?'

'Tonight, when he freed me to marry you.'

'Mona?'

'Yes?'

'Is – is there anyone else in your life?'

She was puzzled. 'Many,' she said at last.

'That you *love*?'

'I love everyone.'

'As – as much as me?'

'Yes.' She seemed to have no idea that this might bother me.

I got off the floor, sat in a chair, and started putting my shoes and socks back on.

'I suppose you – perform – you do what we just did with – other people?'

'*Boko-maru*?'

'*Boko-maru*.'

'Of course.'

'I don't want you to do it with anybody but me from now on,' I declared.

Tears filled her eyes. She adored her promiscuity; was angered that I should try to make her feel shame. 'I make people happy. Love is good, not bad.'

'As your husband, I'll want all your love for myself.'

She stared at me with widening eyes. 'A *sin-wat!*'

'What was that?'

'A *sin-wat!*' she cried. 'A man who wants all of somebody's love. That's very bad.'

'In the case of marriage, I think it's a very good thing. It's the only thing.'

She was still on the floor, and I, now with my shoes and socks back on, was standing. I felt very tall, though I'm not very tall; and I felt very strong, though I'm not very strong; and I was a respectful stranger to my own voice. My voice had a metallic authority that was new.

As I went on talking in ball-peen tones, it dawned on me what was happening, what was happening already. I was already starting to rule.

I told Mona that I had seen her performing a sort of vertical *boko-maru* with a pilot on the reviewing stand shortly after my arrival. 'You are to have nothing more to do with him,' I told her. 'What is his name?'

'I don't even know,' she whispered. She was looking down now.

'And what about young Philip Castle?'

'You mean *boko-maru*?'

'I mean anything and everything. As I understand it, you two grew up together.'

'Yes.'

'Bokonon tutored you both?'

'Yes.' The recollection made her radiant again.

'I suppose there was plenty of *boko-maruing* in those days.'

'Oh, yes!' she said happily.

'You aren't to see him any more, either. Is that clear?'

'No.'

'No?'

'I will not marry a *sin-wat*.' She stood. 'Good-bye.'

'Good-bye?' I was crushed.

'Bokonon tells us it is very wrong not to love everyone exactly the same. What does *your* religion say?'

'I – I don't have one.'

'I *do*.'

I had stopped ruling. 'I see you do,' I said.

'Good-bye, man-with-no-religion.' She went to the stone staircase.

'Mona . . .'

She stopped. 'Yes?'

'Could I have your religion, if I wanted it?'

'Of course.'

'I want it.'

'Good. I love you.'

'And I love you,' I sighed.

## 94 The Highest Mountain

So I became betrothed at dawn to the most beautiful woman in the world. And I agreed to become the next President of San Lorenzo.

'Papa' wasn't dead yet, and it was Frank's feeling that I should get 'Papa's' blessing, if possible. So, as *Borasisi*, the sun, came up, Frank and I drove to 'Papa's' castle in a Jeep we commandeered from the troops guarding the next President.

Mona stayed at Frank's. I kissed her sacredly, and she went to sacred sleep.

Over the mountains Frank and I went, through groves of wild coffee trees, with the flamboyant sunrise on our right.

It was in the sunrise that the cetacean majesty of the highest mountain on the island, of Mount McCabe, made itself known to me. It was a fearful hump, a blue whale, with one queer stone plug on its back for a peak. In scale with a whale, the plug might have been the stump of a snapped harpoon, and it seemed so unrelated to the rest of the mountain that I asked Frank if it had been built by men.

He told me that it was a natural formation. Moreover, he declared that no man, as far as he knew, had ever been to the top of Mount McCabe.

'It doesn't *look* very tough to climb,' I commented. Save for the plug at the top, the mountain presented inclines no more forbidding than court-house steps. And the plug itself, from a distance at any rate, seemed conveniently laced with ramps and ledges.

'Is it sacred or something?' I asked.

'Maybe it was once. But not since Bokonon.'

'Then why hasn't anybody climbed it?'

'Nobody's felt like it yet.'

'Maybe I'll climb it.'

'Go ahead. Nobody's stopping you.'

We rode in silence.

'What *is* sacred to Bokononists?' I asked after a while.

'Not even God, as near as I can tell.'

'Nothing?'

'Just one thing.'

I made some guesses. 'The ocean? The sun?'

'Man,' said Frank. 'That's all. Just man.'


## 95 I See the Hook

We came at last to the castle.

It was low and black and cruel.

Antique cannons still lolled on the battlements. Vines and bird nests clogged the crenels, the machicolations, and the balistrariae.

Its parapets to the north were continuous with the scarp of a monstrous precipice that fell six hundred feet straight down to the lukewarm sea.

It posed the question posed by all such stone piles: how had puny men moved stones so big? And, like all such stone piles, it answered the question itself. Dumb terror had moved those stones so big.

The castle was built according to the wish of Tum-bumwa, Emperor of San Lorenzo, a demented man, an escaped slave. Tum-bumwa was said to have found its design in a child's picture book.

A gory book it must have been.

Just before we reached the palace gate the ruts carried us through a rustic arch made of two telephone poles and a beam that spanned them.

Hanging from the middle of the beam was a huge iron hook. There was a sign impaled on the hook.

'This hook,' the sign proclaimed, 'is reserved for Bokonon himself.'

I turned to look at the hook again, and that thing of sharp iron communicated to me that I really was going to rule. I would chop down the hook!

And I flattered myself that I was going to be a firm, just, and kindly ruler, and that my people would prosper.

Fata Morgana.

Mirage!

## 96 *Bell, Book, and Chicken in a Hatbox*

Frank and I couldn't get right in to see 'Papa'. Dr Schlichter von Koenigswald, the physician in attendance, muttered that we would have to wait about half an hour.

So Frank and I waited in the anteroom of 'Papa's' suite, a room without windows. The room was thirty feet square, furnished with several rugged benches and a card table. The card table supported an electric fan. The walls were stone. There were no pictures, no decorations of any sort on the walls.

There were iron rings fixed to the wall, however, seven feet off the floor and at intervals of six feet. I asked Frank if the room had ever been a torture chamber.

He told me that it had, and that the manhole cover on which I stood was the lid of an oubliette.

There was a listless guard in the ante-room. There was also a Christian minister, who was ready to take care of 'Papa's' spiritual needs as they arose. He had a brass dinner bell and a hatbox with holes drilled in it, and a Bible, and a butcher knife – all laid out on the bench beside him.

He told me there was a live chicken in the hatbox. The chicken was quiet, he said, because he had fed it tranquillizers.

Like all San Lorenzans past the age of twenty-five, he looked at least sixty. He told me that his name was Dr Vox Humana, that he was named after an organ stop that had struck his mother when San Lorenzo Cathedral was dynamited in 1923. His father, he told me without shame, was unknown.

I asked him what particular Christian sect he represented, and I observed frankly that the chicken and the butcher knife were novelties insofar as my understanding of Christianity went.

'The bell,' I commented, 'I can understand how that might fit in nicely.'

He turned out to be an intelligent man. His doctorate, which he invited me to examine, was awarded by the Western Hemisphere University of the Bible of Little Rock, Arkansas. He made contact with the University through a classified ad in *Popular Mechanics*, he told me. He said that the motto of the University had become his own, and that it explained the chicken and the butcher knife. The motto of the University was this:

MAKE RELIGION LIVE!

He said that he had had to feel his way along with Christianity, since Catholicism and Protestantism had been outlawed along with Bokononism.

'So, if I am going to be a Christian under those conditions, I have to make up a lot of new stuff.'

'*Zo,*' he said in dialect, '*yeff jy bam gong be Kret-yeen hooner yoze kon-steez-yen, jy hap my yup oon lot nee stopf.*'

Dr Schlichter von Koenigswald now came out of 'Papa's' suite, looking very German, very tired. 'You can see "Papa" now.'

'We'll be careful not to tire him,' Frank promised.

'If you could kill him,' said von Koenigswald, 'I think he'd be grateful.'

## 97 *The Stinking Christian*

'Papa' Monzano and his merciless disease were in a bed that was made of a golden dinghy – tiller, painter, oarlocks and all, all gilt. His bed was the lifeboat of Bokonon's old schooner, the *Lady's Slipper*; it was the lifeboat of the ship that had brought Bokonon and Corporal McCabe to San Lorenzo so long ago.

The walls of the room were white. But 'Papa' radiated pain so hot and bright that the walls seemed bathed in angry red.

He was stripped from the waist up, and his glistening belly wall was knotted. His belly shivered like a luffing sail.

Around his neck hung a chain with a cylinder the size of a rifle cartridge for a pendant. I supposed that the cylinder contained some magic charm. I was mistaken. It contained a splinter of *ice-nine*.

'Papa' could hardly speak. His teeth chattered and his breathing was beyond control.

'Papa's' agonized head was at the bow of the dinghy, bent back.

Mona's xylophone was near the bed. She had apparently tried to soothe 'Papa' with music the previous evening.

' "Papa"?' whispered Frank.

'Good-bye,' 'Papa' gasped. His eyes were bulging, sightless.

'I brought a friend.'

'Good-bye.'

'He's going to be the next President of San Lorenzo. He'll be a much better president than I could be.'

'Ice!' 'Papa' whimpered.

'He asks for ice,' said von Koenigswald. 'When we bring it, he does not want it.'

'Papa' rolled his eyes. He relaxed his neck, took the weight of his body from the crown of his head. And then he arched his

neck again. 'Does not matter,' he said, 'who is President of . . .'
He did not finish.

I finished for him. 'San Lorenzo?'

'San Lorenzo,' he agreed. He managed a crooked smile.
'Good luck!' he croaked.

'Thank you, sir,' I said.

'Doesn't matter! Bokonon. Get Bokonon.'

I attempted a sophisticated reply to this last. I remembered
that, for the joy of the people, Bokonon was always to be
chased, was never to be caught. 'I will get him.'

'Tell him . . .'

I leaned closer, in order to hear the message from 'Papa' to
Bokonon.

'Tell him I am sorry I did not kill him,' said 'Papa'.

'I will.'

'*You* kill him.'

'Yessir.'

'Papa' gained control enough of his voice to make it com-
manding. 'I mean *really*!'

I said nothing to that. I was not eager to kill anyone.

'He teaches the people lies and lies and lies. Kill him and
teach the people truth.'

'Yessir.'

'You and Hoenikker, you teach them science.'

'Yessir, we will,' I promised.

'Science is magic that *works*.'

He fell silent, relaxed, closed his eyes. And then he whispered,
'Last rites.'

Von Koenigswald called Dr Vox Humana in. Dr Humana
took his tranquillized chicken out of the hatbox, preparing to
administer Christian last rites as he understood them.

'Papa' opened one eye. 'Not you,' he sneered at Dr Humana.
'Get out!'

'Sir?' asked Dr Humana.

'I am a member of the Bokononist faith,' 'Papa' wheezed. 'Get out, you stinking Christian.'

## 98 *Last Rites*

So I was privileged to see the last rites of the Bokononist faith.

We made an effort to find someone among the soldiers and the household staff who would admit that he knew the rites and would give them to 'Papa'. We got no volunteers. That was hardly surprising, with a hook and an oubliette so near.

So Dr von Koenigswald said that he would have a go at the job. He had never administered the rites before, but he had seen Julian Castle do it hundreds of times.

'Are you a Bokononist?' I asked him.

'I agree with one Bokononist idea. I agree that all religions, including Bokononism, are nothing but lies.'

'Will this bother you as a scientist,' I inquired, 'to go through a ritual like this?'

'I am a very bad scientist. I will do anything to make a human being feel better, even if it's unscientific. No scientist worthy of the name could say such a thing.'

And he climbed into the golden boat with 'Papa'. He sat in the stern. Cramped quarters obliged him to have the golden tiller under one arm.

He wore sandals without socks, and he took these off. And then he rolled back the covers at the foot of the bed, exposing 'Papa's' bare feet. He put the soles of his feet against 'Papa's' feet, assuming the classical position for *boko-maru*.

## 99 Dyot meet mat

'*Gott mate mutt*,' crooned Dr von Koenigswald.

'*Dyot meet mat*,' echoed 'Papa' Monzano.

'God made mud,' was what they'd said, each in his own dialect. I will here abandon the dialects of the litany.

'God got lonesome,' said von Koenigswald.

'God got lonesome.'

'So God said to some of the mud, "Sit up!"'

'So God said to some of the mud, "Sit up!"'

'"See all I've made," said God, "the hills, the sea, the sky, the stars."'

'"See all I've made," said God, "the hills, the sea, the sky, the stars."'

'And I was some of the mud that got to sit up and look around.'

'And I was some of the mud that got to sit up and look around.'

'Lucky me, lucky mud.'

'Lucky me, lucky mud.' Tears were streaming down 'Papa's' cheeks.

'I, mud, sat up and saw what a nice job God had done.'

'I, mud, sat up and saw what a nice job God had done.'

'Nice going, God!'

'Nice going, God!' 'Papa' said it with all his heart.

'Nobody but You could have done it, God! I certainly couldn't have.'

'Nobody but You could have done it, God! I certainly couldn't have.'

'I feel very unimportant compared to You.'

'I feel very unimportant compared to You.'

'The only way I can feel the least bit important is to think of all the mud that didn't even get to sit up and look around.'

'The only way I can feel the least bit important is to think of all the mud that didn't even get to sit up and look around.'

'I got so much, and most mud got so little.'

'I got so much, and most mud got so little.'

'*Deng you vore da on-oh!*' cried von Koenigswald.

'*Tz-yenk voo vore lo yon-yo!*' wheezed 'Papa'.

What they had said was, 'Thank you for the honour!'

'Now mud lies down again and goes to sleep.'

'Now mud lies down again and goes to sleep.'

'What memories for mud to have!'

'What memories for mud to have!'

'What interesting other kinds of sitting-up mud I met!'

'What interesting other kinds of sitting-up mud I met!'

'I loved everything I saw!'

'I loved everything I saw!'

'Good night.'

'Good night.'

'I will go to heaven now.'

'I will go to heaven now.'

'I can hardly wait . . .'

'I can hardly wait . . .'

'To find out for certain what my *wampeter* was . . .'

'To find out for certain what my *wampeter* was . . .'

'And who was in my *karass* . . .'

'And who was in my *karass* . . .'

'And all the good things our *karass* did for you.'

'And all the good things our *karass* did for you.'

'Amen.'

'Amen.'

## 100 *Down the Oubliette Goes Frank*

But 'Papa' didn't die and go to heaven – not then.

I asked Frank how we might best time the announcement of my elevation to the Presidency. He was no help, had no ideas; he left it all up to me.

'I thought you were going to back me up,' I complained.

'As far as anything *technical* goes.' Frank was prim about it. I wasn't to violate his integrity as a technician; wasn't to make him exceed the limits of his job.

'I see.'

'However you want to handle people is all right with me. That's *your* responsibility.'

This abrupt abdication of Frank from all human affairs shocked and angered me, and I said to him, meaning to be satirical, 'You mind telling me what, in a purely technical way, is planned for this day of days?'

I got a strictly technical reply. 'Repair the power plant and stage an air show.'

'Good! So one of my first triumphs as President will be to restore electricity to my people.'

Frank didn't see anything funny in that. He gave me a salute. 'I'll try, sir. I'll do my best for you, sir. I can't guarantee how long it'll be before we get juice back.'

'That's what I want – a juicy country.'

'I'll do my best, sir.' Frank saluted me again.

'And the air show?' I asked. 'What's that?'

I got another wooden reply. 'At one o'clock this afternoon, sir, six planes of the San Lorenzan Air Force will fly past the palace here and shoot at targets in the water. It's part of the celebration of the Day of the Hundred Martyrs to Democracy.

The American Ambassador also plans to throw a wreath into the sea.'

So I decided, tentatively, that I would have Frank announce my apotheosis immediately following the wreath ceremony and the air show.

'What do you think of that?' I said to Frank.

'You're the boss, sir.'

'I think I'd better have a speech ready,' I said. 'And there should be some sort of swearing-in, to make it look dignified, official.'

'You're the boss, sir.' Each time he said those words they seemed to come from farther away, as though Frank were descending the rungs of a ladder into a deep shaft, while I was obliged to remain above.

And I realized with chagrin that my agreeing to be boss had freed Frank to do what he wanted to do more than anything else, to do what his father had done: to receive honours and creature comforts while escaping human responsibilities. He was accomplishing this by going down a spiritual oubliette.

## 101 *Like My Predecessors, I Outlaw Bokonon*

So I wrote my speech in a round, bare room at the foot of a tower. There was a table and a chair. And the speech I wrote was round and bare and sparsely furnished, too.

It was hopeful. It was humble.

And I found it impossible not to lean on God. I had never needed such support before, and so had never believed that such support was available.

Now, I found that I had to believe in it – and I did.

In addition, I would need the help of people. I called for a list of the guests who were to be at the ceremonies and found that Julian Castle and his son had not been invited. I sent messengers to invite them at once, since they knew more about my people than anyone, with the exception of Bokonon.

As for Bokonon:

I pondered asking him to join my government, thus bringing about a sort of millennium for my people. And I thought of ordering that the awful hook outside the palace gate be taken down at once, amidst great rejoicing.

But then I understood that a millennium would have to offer something more than a holy man in a position of power, that there would have to be plenty of good things for all to eat, too, and nice places to live for all, and good schools and good health and good times for all, and work for all who wanted it – things Bokonon and I were in no position to provide.

So good and evil had to remain separate; good in the jungle, and evil in the palace. Whatever entertainment there was in that was about all we had to give the people.

There was a knock on my door. A servant told me the guests had begun to arrive.

So I put my speech in my pocket and I mounted the spiral staircase in my tower. I arrived at the uppermost battlement of my castle, and I looked out at my guests, my servants, my cliff, and my lukewarm sea.

## 102  Enemies of Freedom

When I think of all those people on my uppermost battlement, I think of Bokonon's 'hundred-and-nineteenth Calypso', wherein he invites us to sing along with him:

'Where's my good old gang done gone?'
I heard a sad man say.
I whispered in that sad man's ear,
'Your gang's done gone away.'

Present were Ambassador Horlick Minton and his lady;
H. Lowe Crosby, the bicycle manufacturer, and his Hazel; Dr
Julian Castle, humanitarian and philanthropist, and his son,
Philip, author and innkeeper; little Newton Hoenikker, the
picture painter, and his musical sister, Mrs Harrison C. Conners;
my heavenly Mona; Major General Franklin Hoenikker; and
twenty assorted San Lorenzo bureaucrats and military men.

Dead – almost all dead now.

As Bokonon tells us, 'It is never a mistake to say good-bye.'

There was a buffet on my battlements, a buffet burdened
with native delicacies: roasted warblers in little overcoats made
of their own blue-green feathers; lavender land crabs taken from
their shells, minced, fried in coconut oil, and returned to their
shells; fingerling barracuda stuffed with banana paste; and, on
unleavened, unseasoned corn meal wafers, bite-sized cubes of
boiled albatross.

The albatross, I was told, had been shot from the very
bartizan in which the buffet stood.

There were two beverages offered, both un-iced: Pepsi-Cola
and native rum. The Pepsi-Cola was served in plastic Pilseners.
The rum was served in coconut shells. I was unable to identify
the sweet bouquet of the rum, though it somehow reminded
me of early adolescence.

Frank was able to name the bouquet for me. 'Acetone.'

'Acetone?'

'Used in model-airplane cement.'

I did not drink the rum.

Ambassador Minton did a lot of ambassadorial, gourmand

saluting with his coconut, pretending to love all men and all the beverages that sustained them. But I did not see him drink. He had with him, incidentally, a piece of luggage of a sort I had never seen before. It looked like a French horn case, and proved to contain the memorial wreath that was to be cast into the sea.

The only person I saw drink the rum was H. Lowe Crosby, who plainly had no sense of smell. He was having a good time, drinking acetone from his coconut, sitting on a cannon, blocking the touchhole with his big behind. He was looking out to sea through a huge pair of Japanese binoculars. He was looking at targets mounted on bobbing floats anchored offshore.

The targets were cardboard cutouts shaped like men.

They were to be fired upon and bombed in a demonstration of might by the six planes of the San Lorenzan Air Force.

Each target was a caricature of some real person, and the name of that person was painted on the target's back and front.

I asked who the caricaturist was and learned that he was Dr Vox Humana, the Christian minister. He was at my elbow.

'I didn't know you were talented in that direction, too.'

'Oh, yes. When I was a young man, I had a very hard time deciding what to be.'

'I think the choice you made was the right one.'

'I prayed for guidance from Above.'

'You got it.'

H. Lowe Crosby handed his binoculars to his wife. 'There's old Joe Stalin, closest in, and old Fidel Castro's anchored right next to him.'

'And there's old Hitler,' chuckled Hazel, delighted. 'And there's old Mussolini and some old Jap.'

'And there's old Karl Marx.'

'And there's old Kaiser Bill, spiked hat and all,' cooed Hazel. 'I never expected to see *him* again.'

'And there's old Mao. You see old Mao?'

'Isn't *he* gonna get it?' asked Hazel. 'Isn't *he* gonna get the surprise of his life? This sure is a cute idea.'

'They got practically every enemy that freedom ever had out there,' H. Lowe Crosby declared.

## 103 A Medical Opinion on the Effects of a Writer's Strike

None of the guests knew yet that I was to be President. None knew how close to death 'Papa' was. Frank gave out the official word that 'Papa' was resting comfortably, that 'Papa' sent his best wishes to all.

The order of events, as announced by Frank, was that Ambassador Minton would throw his wreath into the sea, in honour of the Hundred Martyrs; and then the airplanes would shoot the targets in the sea; and then he, Frank, would say a few words.

He did not tell the company that, following his speech, there would be a speech by me.

So I was treated as nothing more than a visiting journalist, and I engaged in harmless *granfalloonery* here and there.

'Hello, Mom,' I said to Hazel Crosby.

'Why, if it isn't my boy!' Hazel gave me a perfumed hug, and she told everybody, 'This boy's a Hoosier!'

The Castles, father and son, stood separate from the rest of the company. Long unwelcome at 'Papa's' palace, they were curious as to why they had now been invited there.

Young Castle called me 'Scoop'. 'Good morning, Scoop. What's new in the word game?'

'I might ask the same of you,' I replied.

'I'm thinking of calling a general strike of all writers until mankind finally comes to its senses. Would you support it?'

'Do writers have a right to strike? That would be like the police or firemen walking out.'

'Or the college professors.'

'Or the college professors,' I agreed. I shook my head. 'No, I don't think my conscience would let me support a strike like that. When a man becomes a writer, I think he takes on a sacred obligation to produce beauty and enlightenment and comfort at top speed.'

'I just can't help thinking what a real shaking up it would give people if, all of a sudden, there were no new books, new plays, new histories, new poems . . .'

'And how proud would you be when people started dying like flies?' I demanded.

'They'd die more like mad dogs, I think – snarling and snapping at each other and biting their own tails.'

I turned to Castle the elder. 'Sir, how does a man die when he's deprived of the consolations of literature?'

'In one of two ways,' he said, 'putrescence of the heart or atrophy of the nervous system.'

'Neither one very pleasant, I expect,' I suggested.

'No,' said Castle the elder. 'For the love of God, *both* of you, please keep writing!'


## 104 Sulfathiazole

My heavenly Mona did not approach me and did not encourage me with languishing glances to come to her side. She made a hostess of herself, introducing Angela and little Newt to San Lorenzans.

As I ponder now the meaning of that girl – recall her indifference to 'Papa's' collapse, to her betrothal to me – I vacillate between lofty and cheap appraisals.

Did she represent the highest form of female spirituality?

Or was she anaesthetized, frigid – a cold fish, in fact, a dazed addict of the xylophone, the cult of beauty, and *boko-maru*?

I shall never know.

Bokonon tells us:

> A lover's a liar,
> To himself he lies.
> The truthful are loveless,
> Like oysters their eyes!

So my instructions are clear, I suppose. I am to remember my Mona as having been sublime.

'Tell me,' I appealed to young Philip Castle on the Day of the Hundred Martyrs to Democracy, 'have you spoken to your friend and admirer, H. Lowe Crosby, today?'

'He didn't recognize me with a suit and shoes and necktie on,' young Castle replied. 'We've already had a nice talk about bicycles. We may have another.'

I found that I was no longer amused by Crosby's wanting to build bicycles in San Lorenzo. As chief executive of the island I wanted a bicycle factory very much. I developed sudden respect for what H. Lowe Crosby was and could do.

'How do you think the people of San Lorenzo would take to industrialization?' I asked the Castles, father and son.

'The people of San Lorenzo,' the father told me, 'are interested in only three things: fishing, fornication, and Bokononism.'

'Don't you think they could be interested in progress?'

'They've seen some of it. There's only one aspect of progress that really excites them.'

'What's that?'

'The electric guitar.'

I excused myself and I rejoined the Crosbys.

Frank Hoenikker was with them, explaining who Bokonon was and what he was against. 'He's against science.'

'How can anybody in his right mind be against science?' asked Crosby.

'I'd be dead now if it wasn't for penicillin,' said Hazel. 'And so would my mother.'

'How old *is* your mother?' I inquired.

'A hundred and six. Isn't that wonderful?'

'It certainly is,' I agreed.

'And I'd be a widow, too, if it wasn't for the medicine they gave my husband that time,' said Hazel. She had to ask her husband the name of the medicine. 'Honey, what was the name of that stuff that saved your life that time?'

'Sulfathiazole.'

And I made the mistake of taking an albatross canapé from a passing tray.

## 105 *Pain-killer*

As it happened – 'As it was *supposed* to happen,' Bokonon would say – albatross meat disagreed with me so violently that I was ill the moment I'd choked the first piece down. I was compelled to canter down the stone spiral staircase in search of a bathroom. I availed myself of one adjacent to 'Papa's' suite.

When I shuffled out, somewhat relieved, I was met by Dr Schlichter von Koenigswald, who was bounding from 'Papa's' bedroom. He had a wild look, and he took me by the arms and he cried, 'What is it? What was it he had hanging around his neck?'

'I beg your pardon?'

'He took it! Whatever was in that cylinder, "Papa" took – and now he's dead.'

I remembered the cylinder 'Papa' had hung around his neck, and I made an obvious guess as to its contents. 'Cyanide?'

'Cyanide? Cyanide turns a man to cement in a second?'

'Cement?'

'Marble! Iron! I have never seen such a rigid corpse before. Strike it anywhere and you get a note like a marimba! Come look!' Von Koenigswald hustled me into 'Papa's' bedroom.

In the bed, in the golden dinghy, was a hideous thing to see. 'Papa' was dead, but his was not a corpse to which one could say, 'At rest at last.'

'Papa's' head was bent back as far as it would go. His weight rested on the crown of his head and the soles of his feet, with the rest of his body forming a bridge whose arch thrust towards the ceiling. He was shaped like an andiron.

That he had died of the contents of the cylinder around his neck was obvious. One hand held the cylinder and the cylinder was uncapped. And the thumb and index finger of the other had, as though having just released a little pinch of something, were stuck between his teeth.

Dr von Koenigswald slipped the tholepin of an oarlock from its socket in the gunwale of the gilded dinghy. He tapped 'Papa' on his belly with the steel oarlock, and 'Papa' really did make a sound like a marimba.

And 'Papa's' lips and nostrils and eyeballs were glazed with a blue-white frost.

Such a syndrome is no novelty now, God knows. But it certainly was then. 'Papa' Monzano was the first man in history to die of *ice-nine*.

I record that fact for whatever it may be worth. 'Write it all down,' Bokonon tells us. He is really telling us, of course, how futile it is to write or read histories. 'Without accurate records of the past, how can men and women be expected to avoid making serious mistakes in the future?' he asks ironically.

So, again: 'Papa' Monzano was the first man in history to die of *ice-nine*.

## 106 What Bokononists Say When They Commit Suicide

Dr von Koenigswald, the humanitarian with the terrible deficit of Auschwitz in his kindliness account, was the second to die of *ice-nine*.

He was talking about rigor mortis, a subject I had introduced.

'Rigor mortis does not set in in seconds,' he declared. 'I turned my back to "Papa" for just a moment. He was raving . . .'

'What about?' I asked.

'Pain, ice, Mona – everything. And then "Papa" said, "Now I will destroy the whole world."'

'What did he mean by that?'

'It's what Bokononists always say when they are about to commit suicide.' Von Koenigswald went to a basin of water, meaning to wash his hands. 'When I turned to look at him,' he told me, his hands poised over the water, 'he was dead – as hard as a statue, just as you see him. I brushed my fingers over his lips. They looked so peculiar.'

He put his hands into the water. 'What chemical could possibly . . .' The question trailed off.

Von Koenigswald raised his hands, and the water in the basin came with them. It was no longer water, but a hemisphere of *ice-nine*.

Von Koenigswald touched the tip of his tongue to the blue-white mystery.

Frost bloomed on his lips. He froze solid, tottered, and crashed.

The blue-white hemisphere shattered. Chunks skittered over the floor.

I went to the door and bawled for help.

Soldiers and servants came running.

I ordered them to bring Frank and Newt and Angela to 'Papa's' room at once.

At last I had seen *ice-nine*!

## 107 *Feast Your Eyes!*

I let the three children of Dr Felix Hoenikker into 'Papa' Monzano's bedroom. I closed the door and put my back to it. My mood was bitter and grand. I knew *ice-nine* for what it was. I had seen it often in my dreams.

There could be no doubt that Frank had given 'Papa' *ice-nine*. And it seemed certain that if *ice-nine* were Frank's to give, then it was Angela's and little Newt's to give, too.

So I snarled at all three, called them to account for monstrous criminality. I told them that the jig was up, that I knew about them and *ice-nine*. I tried to alarm them about *ice-nine*'s being a means to ending life on earth. I was so impressive that they never thought to ask how I knew about *ice-nine*.

'Feast your eyes!' I said.

Well, as Bokonon tells us: 'God never wrote a good play in

His Life.' The scene in 'Papa's' room did not lack for spectacular issues and props, and my opening speech was the right one.

But the first reply from a Hoenikker destroyed all magnificence.

Little Newt threw up.

## 108 Frank Tells Us What to Do

And then we all wanted to throw up.

Newt certainly did what was called for.

'I couldn't agree more,' I told Newt. And I snarled at Angela and Frank, 'Now that we've got Newt's opinion, I'd like to hear what you two have to say.'

'Uck,' said Angela, cringing, her tongue out. She was the colour of putty.

'Are those your sentiments, too?' I asked Frank. '"Uck?" General, is that what you say?'

Frank had his teeth bared, and his teeth were clenched, and he was breathing shallowly and whistlingly between them.

'Like the dog,' murmured little Newt, looking down at Von Koenigswald.

'What dog?'

Newt whispered his answer, and there was scarcely any wind behind the whisper. But such were the acoustics of the stonewalled room that we had all heard the whisper as clearly as we would have heard the chiming of a crystal bell.

'Christmas Eve, when Father died.'

Newt was talking to himself. And, when I asked him to tell me about the dog on the night his father died, he looked up at me as though I had intruded on a dream. He found me irrelevant.

His brother and sister, however, belonged in the dream. And he talked to his brother in that nightmare; told Frank, 'You gave it to him.

'That's how you got this fancy job, isn't it?' Newt asked Frank wonderingly. 'What did you tell him – that you had something better than the hydrogen bomb?'

Frank didn't acknowledge the question. He was looking around the room intently, taking it all in. He unclenched his teeth, and he made them click rapidly, blinking his eyes with every click. His colour was coming back. This is what he said.

'Listen, we've got to clean up this mess.'

## 109  Frank Defends Himself

'General,' I told Frank, 'that must be one of the most cogent statements made by a major general this year. As my technical advisor, how do you recommend that *we*, as you put it so well, "clean up this mess"?'

Frank gave me a straight answer. He snapped his fingers. I could see him dissociating himself from the causes of the mess; identifying himself, with growing pride and energy, with the purifiers, the world-savers, the cleaners-up.

'Brooms, dustpans, blowtorch, hot plate, buckets,' he commanded, snapping, snapping, snapping his fingers.

'You propose applying a blowtorch to the bodies?' I asked.

Frank was so charged with technical thinking now that he was practically tap dancing to the music of his fingers. 'We'll sweep up the big pieces on the floor, melt them in a bucket on a hot plate. Then we'll go over every square inch of floor with a blowtorch, in case there are any microscopic crystals. What we'll do with the bodies – and the bed . . .' He had to think some more.

'A funeral pyre!' he cried, really pleased with himself. 'I'll have a great big funeral pyre built out by the hook, and we'll have the bodies and bed carried out and thrown on.'

He started to leave, to order the pyre built and to get the things we needed in order to clean up the room.

Angela stopped him. 'How *could* you?' she wanted to know.

Frank gave her a glassy smile. 'Everything's going to be all right.'

'How *could* you give it to a man like "Papa" Monzano?' Angela asked him.

'Let's clean up the mess first; then we can talk.'

Angela had him by the arms, and she wouldn't let him go. 'How *could* you!' She shook him.

Frank pried his sister's hands from himself. His glassy smile went away and he turned sneeringly nasty for a moment – a moment in which he told her with all possible contempt, 'I bought myself a job, just the way you bought yourself a tomcat husband, just the way Newt bought himself a week on Cape Cod with a Russian midget!'

The glassy smile returned.

Frank left; and he slammed the door.

## 110 The Fourteenth Book

'Sometimes the *pool-pah*,' Bokonon tells us, 'exceeds the power of humans to comment.' Bokonon translates *pool-pah* at one point in *The Books of Bokonon* as 'shit storm' and at another point as 'wrath of God'.

From what Frank had said before he slammed the door,

I gathered that the Republic of San Lorenzo and the three Hoenikkers weren't the only ones who had *ice-nine*. Apparently the United States of America and the Union of Soviet Socialist Republics had it, too. The United States had obtained it through Angela's husband, whose plant in Indianapolis was understandably surrounded by electrified fences and homicidal German shepherds. And Soviet Russia had come by it through Newt's little Zinka, that winsome troll of Ukrainian ballet.

I was without comment.

I bowed my head and closed my eyes; and I awaited Frank's return with the humble tools it would take to clean up one bedroom – one bedroom out of all the bedrooms in the world, a bedroom infested with *ice-nine*.

Somewhere, in that violet, velvet oblivion, I heard Angela say something to me. It wasn't in her own defence. It was in defence of little Newt. 'Newt didn't give it to her. She *stole* it.'

I found the explanation uninteresting.

'What hope can there be for mankind,' I thought, 'when there are such men as Felix Hoenikker to give such playthings as *ice-nine* to such short-sighted children as almost all men and women are?'

And I remembered *The Fourteenth Book of Bokonon*, which I had read in its entirety the night before. *The Fourteenth Book* is entitled, 'What Can a Thoughtful Man Hope for Mankind on Earth, Given the Experience of the Past Million Years?'

It doesn't take long to read *The Fourteenth Book*. It consists of one word and a period.

This is it:

'Nothing.'

## III *Time Out*

Frank came back with brooms and dustpans, a blowtorch, and a kerosene hot plate, and a good old bucket and rubber gloves.

We put on the gloves in order not to contaminate our hands with *ice-nine*. Frank set the hot plate on the heavenly Mona's xylophone and put the honest old bucket on top of that.

And we picked up the bigger chunks of *ice-nine* from the floor; and we dropped them into that humble bucket; and they melted. They became good old, sweet old, honest old water.

Angela and I swept the floor, and little Newt looked under furniture for bits of *ice-nine* we might have missed. And Frank followed our sweeping with the purifying flame of the torch.

The brainless serenity of charwomen and janitors working late at night came over us. In a messy world we were at least making our little corner clean.

And I heard myself asking Newt and Angela and Frank in conversational tones to tell me about the Christmas Eve on which the old man died, to tell me about the dog.

And, childishly sure that they were making everything all right by cleaning up, the Hoenikkers told me the tale.

The tale went like this:

On that fateful Christmas Eve, Angela went into the village for Christmas tree lights, and Newt and Frank went for a walk on the lonely winter beach, where they met a black Labrador retriever. The dog was friendly, as all Labrador retrievers are, and he followed Frank and little Newt home.

Felix Hoenikker died – died in his white wicker chair looking out at the sea – while his children were gone. All day the old man had been teasing his children with hints about *ice-nine*, showing it to them in a little bottle on whose label he had drawn a skull and crossbones, and on whose label he had written: 'Danger! *Ice-nine*! Keep away from moisture!'

All day long the old man had been nagging his children with words like these, merry in tone: 'Come on now, stretch your minds a little. I've told you that its melting point is a hundred and fourteen point four degrees Fahrenheit, and I've told you that it's composed of nothing but hydrogen and oxygen. What could the explanation be? Think a little! Don't be afraid of straining your brains. They won't break.'

'He was always telling us to stretch our brains,' said Frank, recalling olden times.

'I gave up trying to stretch my brain when I-don't-know-how-old-I-was,' Angela confessed, leaning on her broom. 'I couldn't even listen to him when he talked about science. I'd just nod and pretend I was trying to stretch my brain, but that poor brain, as far as science went, didn't have any more stretch than an old garter belt.'

Apparently, before he sat down in his wicker chair and died, the old man played puddly games in the kitchen with water and pots and pans and *ice-nine*. He must have been converting water to *ice-nine* and back to water again, for every pot and pan was out on the kitchen countertops. A meat thermometer was out, too, so the old man must have been taking the temperature of things.

The old man meant to take only a brief time out in his chair, for he left quite a mess in the kitchen. Part of the disorder was a saucepan filled with solid *ice-nine*. He no doubt meant to melt it up, to reduce the world's supply of the blue-white stuff to a splinter in a bottle again – after a brief time out.

But, as Bokonon tells us, 'Any man can call time out, but no man can say how long the time out will be.'

## 112 *Newt's Mother's Reticule*

'I should have known he was dead the minute I came in,' said Angela, leaning on her broom again. 'That wicker chair, it wasn't making a sound. It always talked, creaked away, when Father was in it – even when he was asleep.'

But Angela had assumed that her father was sleeping, and she went on to decorate the Christmas tree.

Newt and Frank came in with the Labrador retriever. They went out into the kitchen to find something for the dog to eat. They found the old man's puddles.

There was water on the floor, and little Newt took a dishrag and wiped it up. He tossed the sopping dishrag onto the counter.

As it happened, the dishrag fell into the pan containing *ice-nine*.

Frank thought the pan contained some sort of cake frosting, and he held it down to Newt, to show Newt what his carelessness with the dishrag had done.

Newt peeled the dishrag from the surface and found that the dishrag had a peculiar, metallic, snaky quality, as though it were made of finely-woven gold mesh.

'The reason I say "gold mesh",' said little Newt, there in 'Papa's' bedroom, 'is that it reminded me right away of Mother's reticule, of how the reticule felt.'

Angela explained sentimentally that when a child, Newt had treasured his mother's gold reticule. I gathered that it was a little evening bag.

'It felt so funny to me, like nothing else I'd ever touched,' said Newt, investigating his old fondness for the reticule. 'I wonder whatever happened to it.'

'I wonder what happened to a *lot* of things,' said Angela. The question echoed back through time – woeful, lost.

What happened to the dishrag that felt like a reticule, at any rate, was that Newt held it out to the dog, and the dog licked it. And the dog froze stiff.

Newt went to tell his father about the stiff dog and found out that his father was stiff, too.

## 113 *History*

Our work in 'Papa's' bedroom was done at last.

But the bodies still had to be carried to the funeral pyre. We decided that this should be done with pomp, that we should put it off until the ceremonies in honour of the Hundred Martyrs to Democracy were over.

The last thing we did was stand von Koenigswald on his feet in order to decontaminate the place where he had been lying. And then we hid him, standing up, in 'Papa's' clothes closet.

I'm not quite sure why we hid him. I think it must have been to simplify the tableau.

As for Newt's and Angela's and Frank's tale of how they divided up the world's supply of *ice-nine* on Christmas Eve – it petered out when they got to details of the crime itself. The Hoenikkers couldn't remember that anyone said anything to justify their taking *ice-nine* as personal property. They talked about what *ice-nine* was, recalling the old man's brain-stretchers, but there was no talk of morals.

'Who did the dividing?' I inquired.

So thoroughly had the three Hoenikkers obliterated their memories of the incident that it was difficult for them to give me even that fundamental detail.

'It wasn't Newt,' said Angela at last. 'I'm sure of that.'

'It was either you or me,' mused Frank, thinking hard.

'You got the three Mason jars off the kitchen shelf,' said Angela. 'It wasn't until the next day that we got the three little Thermos jugs.'

'That's right,' Frank agreed. 'And then you took an ice pick and chipped up the *ice-nine* in the saucepan.'

'That's right,' said Angela. 'I did. And then somebody brought tweezers from the bathroom.'

Newt raised his little hand. 'I did.'

Angela and Newt were amazed, remembering how enterprising little Newt had been.

'I was the one who picked up the chips and put them in the Mason jars,' Newt recounted. He didn't bother to hide the swagger he must have felt.

'What did you people do with the dog?' I asked limply.

'We put him in the oven,' Frank told me. 'It was the only thing to do.'

'History!' writes Bokonon. 'Read it and weep!'

## 114 *When I Felt the Bullet Enter My Heart*

So I once again mounted the spiral staircase in my tower; once again arrived at the uppermost battlement of my castle; and once more looked out at my guests, my servants, my cliff, and my lukewarm sea.

The Hoenikkers were with me. We had locked 'Papa's' door, and had spread the word among the household staff that 'Papa' was feeling much better.

Soldiers were now building a funeral pyre out by the hook. They did not know what the pyre was for.

There were many, many secrets that day.

Busy, busy, busy.

I supposed that the ceremonies might as well begin, and I told Frank to suggest to Ambassador Horlick Minton that he deliver his speech.

Ambassador Minton went to the seaward parapet with his memorial wreath still in its case. And he delivered an amazing speech in honour of the Hundred Martyrs to Democracy. He dignified the dead, their country, and the life that was over for them by saying the 'Hundred Martyrs to Democracy' in island dialect. That fragment of dialect was graceful and easy on his lips.

The rest of his speech was in American English. He had a written speech with him – fustian and bombast, I imagine. But, when he found he was going to speak to so few, and to fellow Americans for the most part, he put the formal speech away.

A light sea wind ruffled his thinning hair. 'I am about to do a very un-ambassadorial thing,' he declared. 'I am about to tell you what I really feel.'

Perhaps Minton had inhaled too much acetone, or perhaps he had an inkling of what was about to happen to everybody but me. At any rate, it was a strikingly Bokononist speech he gave.

'We are gathered here, friends,' he said, 'to honour *lo Hoon-yera Mora-toorz tut Zamoo-cratz-ya*, children dead, all dead, all murdered in war. It is customary on days like this to call such lost children *men*. I am unable to call them men for this simple reason: that in the same war in which *lo Hoon-yera Mora-toorz tut Zamoo-cratz-ya* died, my own son died.

'My soul insists that I mourn not a man but a child.

'I do not say that children at war do not die like men, if they have to die. To their everlasting honour and our everlasting shame, they *do* die like men, thus making possible the manly jubilation of patriotic holidays.

'But they are murdered children all the same.

'And I propose to you that if we are to pay our sincere respects to the hundred lost children of San Lorenzo, that we might best spend the day despising what killed them; which is to say, the stupidity and viciousness of all mankind.

'Perhaps, when we remember wars, we should take off our clothes and paint ourselves blue and go on all fours all day long and grunt like pigs. That would surely be more appropriate than noble oratory and shows of flags and well-oiled guns.

'I do not mean to be ungrateful for the fine, martial show we are about to see – and a thrilling show it really will be . . .'

He looked each of us in the eye, and then he commented very softly, throwing it away, 'And hooray say I for thrilling shows.'

We had to strain our ears to hear what Minton said next.

'But if today is really in honour of a hundred children murdered in war,' he said, 'is today a day for a thrilling show?

'The answer is yes, on one condition: that we, the celebrants, are working consciously and tirelessly to reduce the stupidity and viciousness of ourselves and of all mankind.'

He unsnapped the catches on his wreath case.

'See what I have brought?' he asked us.

He opened the case and showed us the scarlet lining and the golden wreath. The wreath was made of wire and artificial laurel leaves, and the whole was sprayed with radiator paint.

The wreath was spanned by a cream-coloured silk ribbon on which was printed, 'PRO PATRIA'.

Minton now recited a poem from Edgar Lee Masters' *Spoon River Anthology*, a poem that must have been incomprehensible to the San Lorenzans in the audience – and to H. Lowe Crosby and his Hazel, too, for that matter, and to Angela and Frank.

I was the first fruits of the battle of Missionary Ridge.
When I felt the bullet enter my heart
I wished I had staid at home and gone to jail
For stealing the hogs of Curl Trenary,
Instead of running away and joining the army.
Rather a thousand times the county jail
Than to lie under this marble figure with wings,
And this granite pedestal
Bearing the words, *'Pro Patria'*.
What do they mean, anyway?

'What do they mean, anyway?' echoed Ambassador Horlick Minton. 'They mean, "For one's country".' And he threw away another line. 'Any country at all,' he murmured.

'This wreath I bring is a gift from the people of one country to the people of another. Never mind which countries. Think of people . . .

'And children murdered in war . . .

'And any country at all.

'Think of peace.

'Think of brotherly love.

'Think of plenty.

'Think of what a paradise this world would be if men were kind and wise.

'As stupid and vicious as men are, this is a lovely day,' said Ambassador Horlick Minton. 'I, in my own heart and as a representative of the peace-loving people of the United States of America, pity *lo Hoon-year Mora-toorz tut Zamoo-cratz-ya* for being dead on this fine day.'

And he sailed the wreath off the parapet.

There was a hum in the air. The six planes of the San Lorenzan Air Force were coming, skimming my lukewarm sea. They were going to shoot the effigies of what H. Lowe

Crosby had called 'practically every enemy that freedom ever had'.

## 115  As It Happened

We went to the seaward parapet to see the show. The planes were no larger than grains of black pepper. We were able to spot them because one, as it happened, was trailing smoke.

We supposed that smoke was part of the show.

I stood next to H. Lowe Crosby, who, as it happened, was alternately eating albatross and drinking native rum. He exhaled fumes of model airplane cement between lips glistening with albatross fat. My recent nausea returned.

I withdrew to the landward parapet alone, gulping air. There were sixty feet of old stone pavement between me and all the rest.

I saw the planes would be coming in low, below the footings of the castle, and that I would miss the show. But nausea made me incurious. I turned my head in the direction of their now snarling approach. Just as their guns began to hammer, one plane, the one that had been trailing smoke, suddenly appeared, belly up, in flames.

It dropped from my line of sight again and crashed at once into the cliff below the castle. Its bombs and fuel exploded.

The surviving planes went booming on, their racket thinning down to a mosquito hum.

And then there was the sound of a rockslide – and one great tower of 'Papa's' castle, undermined, crashed down to the sea.

The people on the seaward parapet looked in astonishment at the empty socket where the tower had stood. Then I could hear rockslides of all sizes in a conversation that was almost orchestral.

The conversation went very fast, and new voices entered in. They were the voices of the castle's timbers lamenting that their burdens were becoming too great.

And then a crack crossed the battlement like lightning, ten feet from my curling toes.

It separated me from my fellow men.

The castle groaned and wept aloud.

The others comprehended their peril. They, along with tons of masonry, were about to lurch out and down. Although the crack was only a foot wide, people began to cross it with heroic leaps.

Only my complacent Mona crossed the crack with a simple step.

The crack gnashed shut; opened wider, leeringly. Still trapped on the canted deathtrap were H. Lowe Crosby and his Hazel and Ambassador Horlick Minton and his Claire.

Philip Castle and Frank and I reached across the abyss to haul the Crosbys to safety. Our arms were now extended imploringly to the Mintons.

Their expressions were bland. I can only guess what was going through their minds. My guess is that they were thinking of dignity, of emotional proportion above all else.

Panic was not their style. I doubt that suicide was their style either. But their good manners killed them, for the doomed crescent of castle now moved away from us like an ocean liner moving away from a dock.

The image of a voyage seems to have occurred to the voyaging Mintons, too, for they waved to us with a wan amiability.

They held hands.

They faced the sea.

Out they went; then down they went in a cataclysmic rush, were gone!

## 116 The Grand Ah-whoom

The ragged rim of oblivion was now inches from my curling toes. I looked down. My lukewarm sea had swallowed all. A lazy curtain of dust was wafting out to sea, the only trace of all that fell.

The palace, its massive, seaward mask now gone, greeted the north with a leper's smile, snaggle-toothed and bristly. The bristles were the splintered ends of timbers. Immediately below me a large chamber had been laid open. The floor of that chamber, unsupported, stabbed out into space like a diving platform.

I dreamed for a moment of dropping to the platform, of springing up from it in a breath-taking swan dive, of folding my arms, of knifing downward into a blood-warm eternity with never a splash.

I was recalled from this dream by the cry of a darting bird above me. It seemed to be asking me what had happened. 'Poo-tee-phweet?' it asked.

We all looked up at the bird, and then at one another.

We backed away from the abyss, full of dread. And, when I stepped off the paving stone that had supported me, the stone began to rock. It was no more stable than a teeter-totter. And it tottered now over the diving platform.

Down it crashed onto the platform, made the platform a chute. And down the chute came the furnishings still remaining in the room below.

A xylophone shot out first, scampering fast on its tiny wheels.

Out came a bedside table in a crazy race with a bounding blowtorch. Out came chairs in hot pursuit.

And somewhere in that room below, out of sight, something mightily reluctant to move was beginning to move.

Down the chute it crept. At last it showed its golden bow. It was the boat in which dead 'Papa' lay.

It reached the end of the chute. Its bow nodded. Down it tipped. Down it fell, end over end.

'Papa' was thrown clear, and he fell separately.

I closed my eyes.

There was a sound like that of the gentle closing of a portal as big as the sky, the great door of heaven being closed softly. It was a grand AH-WHOOM.

I opened my eyes – and all the sea was *ice-nine*.

The moist green earth was a blue-white pearl.

The sky darkened. *Borasisi*, the sun, became a sickly yellow ball, tiny and cruel.

The sky was filled with worms. The worms were tornadoes.

## 117 *Sanctuary*

I looked up at the sky where the bird had been. An enormous worm with a violet mouth was directly overhead. It buzzed like bees. It swayed. With obscene peristalsis, it ingested air.

We humans separated; fled my shattered battlements; tumbled down staircases on the landward side.

Only H. Lowe Crosby and his Hazel cried out. 'American! American!' they cried, as though tornadoes were interested in the *granfalloons* to which their victims belonged.

I could not see the Crosbys. They had descended by another staircase. Their cries and the sounds of others, panting and running, came gabbling to me through a corridor of the castle. My only companion was my heavenly Mona, who had followed noiselessly.

When I hesitated, she slipped past me and opened the door to the anteroom of 'Papa's' suite. The walls and roof of the anteroom were gone. But the stone floor remained. And in its centre was the manhole cover of the oubliette. Under the wormy sky, in the flickering violet light from the mouths of tornadoes that wished to eat us, I lifted the cover.

The oesophagus of the dungeon was fitted with iron rungs. I replaced the manhole cover from within. Down those iron rungs we went.

And at the foot of the ladder we found a state secret. 'Papa' Monzano had caused a cosy bomb shelter to be constructed there. It had a ventilation shaft, with a fan driven by a stationary bicycle. A tank of water was recessed in one wall. The water was sweet and wet, as yet untainted by *ice-nine*. And there was a chemical toilet, and a short-wave radio, and a Sears, Roebuck catalogue; and there were cases of delicacies, and liquor, and candles; and there were bound copies of the *National Geographic* going back twenty years.

And there was a set of *The Books of Bokonon*.

And there were twin beds.

I lighted a candle. I opened a can of Campbell's chicken gumbo soup and I put it on a Sterno stove. And I poured two glasses of Virgin Islands rum.

Mona sat on one bed. I sat on the other.

'I am about to say something that must have been said by men to women several times before,' I informed her. 'However, I don't believe that these words have ever carried quite the freight they carry now.'

'Oh?'

I spread my hands. 'Here we are.'

## 118 *The Iron Maiden and the Oubliette*

*The Sixth Book* of *The Books of Bokonon* is devoted to pain, in particular to tortures inflicted by men on men. 'If I am ever put to death on the hook,' Bokonon warns us, 'expect a very human performance.'

Then he speaks of the rack and the peddiwinkus and the iron maiden and the *veglia* and the oubliette.

> In any case, there's bound to be much crying.
> But the oubliette alone will let you think while dying.

And so it was in Mona's and my rock womb. At least we could think. And one thing I thought was that the creature comforts of the dungeon did nothing to mitigate the basic fact of oubliation.

During our first day and night underground, tornadoes rattled our manhole cover many times an hour. Each time the pressure in our hole would drop suddenly, and our ears would pop and our heads would ring.

As for the radio – there was crackling, fizzing static and that was all. From one end of the short-wave band to the other not one word, not one telegrapher's beep, did I hear. If life still existed here and there, it did not broadcast.

Nor does life broadcast to this day.

This I assumed: tornadoes, strewing the poisonous blue-white frost of *ice-nine* everywhere, tore everyone and everything above the ground to pieces. Anything that still lived would die soon enough of thirst – or hunger – or rage – or apathy.

I turned to *The Books of Bokonon*, still sufficiently unfamiliar with them to believe that they contained spiritual comfort somewhere. I passed quickly over the warning on the title page of *The First Book*:

Don't be a fool! Close this book at once! It is nothing but *foma*!

*Foma*, of course, are lies.
And then I read this:

In the beginning, God created the earth, and he looked upon it in His cosmic loneliness.

And God said, 'Let Us make living creatures out of mud, so the mud can see what We have done.' And God created every living creature that now moveth, and one was man. Mud as man alone could speak. God leaned close as mud as man sat up, looked around, and spoke. Man blinked. 'What is the *purpose* of all this?' he asked politely.

'Everything must have a purpose?' asked God.

'Certainly,' said man.

'Then I leave it to you to think of one for all this,' said God. And He went away.

I thought this was trash.

'Of course it's trash!' says Bokonon.

And I turned to my heavenly Mona for comforting secrets a good deal more profound.

I was able, while mooning at her across the space that separated our beds, to imagine that behind her marvellous eyes lurked mysteries as old as Eve.

I will not go into the sordid sex episode that followed. Suffice it to say that I was both repulsive and repulsed.

The girl was not interested in reproduction – hated the idea. Before the tussle was over, I was given full credit by her, and by myself, too, for having invented the whole bizarre, grunting, sweating enterprise by which new human beings were made.

Returning to my own bed, gnashing my teeth, I supposed that she honestly had no idea what love-making was all about. But then she said to me, gently, 'It would be very sad to have a little baby now. Don't you agree?'

'Yes,' I agreed murkily.

'Well, that's the way little babies are made, in case you didn't know.'

## 119 *Mona Thanks Me*

'Today I will be a Bulgarian Minister of Education,' Bokonon tells us. 'Tomorrow I will be Helen of Troy.' His meaning is crystal clear: Each one of us has to be what he or she is. And, down in the oubliette, that was mainly what I thought – with the help of *The Books of Bokonon*.

Bokonon invited me to sing along with him:

> We do, doodley do, doodley do, doodley do,
> What we must, muddily must, muddily must, muddily must;
> Muddily do, muddily do, muddily do, muddily do,
> Until we bust, bodily bust, bodily bust, bodily bust.

I made up a tune to go with that and I whistled it under my breath as I drove the bicycle that drove the fan that gave us air, good old air.

'Man breathes in oxygen and exhales carbon dioxide,' I called to Mona.

'What?'

'Science.'

'Oh.'

'One of the secrets of life man was a long time understanding:
Animals breathe in what animals breathe out, and vice versa.'

'I didn't know.'

'You know now.'

'Thank you.'

'You're welcome.'

When I'd bicycled our atmosphere to sweetness and fresh-
ness, I dismounted and climbed the iron rungs to see what the
weather was like above. I did that several times a day. On that
day, the fourth, I perceived through the narrow crescent of the
lifted manhole cover that the weather had become somewhat
stabilized.

The stability was of a wildly dynamic sort, for the tornadoes
were as numerous as ever, and tornadoes remain numerous to
this day. But their mouths no longer gobbled and gnashed at the
earth. The mouths in all directions were discreetly withdrawn to
an altitude of perhaps a half of a mile. And their altitude varied
so little from moment to moment that San Lorenzo might have
been protected by a tornado-proof sheet of glass.

We let three more days go by, making certain that the
tornadoes had become as sincerely reticent as they seemed.
And then we filled canteens from our water tank and we went
above.

The air was dry and hot and deathly still.

I had heard it suggested one time that the seasons in the
temperate zone ought to be six rather than four in number:
summer, autumn, locking, winter, unlocking, and spring. And
I remembered that as I straightened up beside our manhole,
and stared and listened and sniffed.

There were no smells. There was no movement. Every step
I took made a gravelly squeak in blue-white frost. And every

squeak was echoed loudly. The season of locking was over. The earth was locked up tight.

It was winter, now and forever.

I helped my Mona out of our hole. I warned her to keep her hands away from the blue-white frost and to keep her hands away from her mouth, too. 'Death has never been quite so easy to come by,' I told her. 'All you have to do is touch the ground and then your lips and you're done for.'

She shook her head and sighed. 'A very bad mother.'

'What?'

'Mother Earth – she isn't a very good mother any more.'

'Hello? Hello?' I called through the palace ruins. The awesome winds had torn canyons through that great stone pile. Mona and I made a half-hearted search for survivors – half-hearted because we could sense no life. Not even a nibbling, twinkle-nosed rat had survived.

The arch of the palace gate was the only man-made form untouched. Mona and I went to it. Written at its base in white paint was a Bokononist 'Calypso'. The lettering was neat. It was new. It was proof that someone else had survived the winds.

The 'Calypso' was this:

> Someday, someday, this crazy world will have to end,
> And our God will take things back that He to us did lend.
> And if, on that sad day, you want to scold our God,
> Why go right ahead and scold Him. He'll just smile and nod.

## 120  *To Whom It May Concern*

I recalled an advertisement for a set of children's books called *The Book of Knowledge*. In that ad, a trusting boy and girl looked up at their father. 'Daddy,' one asked, 'what makes the sky blue?' The answer, presumably, could be found in *The Book of Knowledge*.

If I had had a daddy beside me as Mona and I walked down the road from the palace, I would have had plenty of questions to ask as I clung to his hand. 'Daddy, why are all the trees broken? Daddy, why are all the birds dead? Daddy, what makes the sky so sick and wormy? Daddy, what makes the sea so hard and still?'

It occurred to me that I was better qualified to answer those tough questions than any other human being, provided there were any other human beings alive. In case anyone was, I knew what had gone wrong – where and how.

So what?

I wondered where the dead could be. Mona and I ventured more than a mile from our oubliette without seeing one dead human being.

I wasn't half so curious about the living, probably because I sensed accurately that I would first have to contemplate a lot of dead. I saw no columns of smoke from possible campfires; but they would have been hard to see against an horizon of worms.

One thing did catch my eye: a lavender corona about the queer plug that was the peak on the hump of Mount McCabe. It seemed to be calling me, and I had a silly, cinematic notion of climbing that peak with Mona. But what would it mean?

We were walking into the wrinkles now at the foot of Mount McCabe. And Mona, as though aimlessly, left my side, left the road, and climbed one of the wrinkles. I followed.

I joined her at the top of the ridge. She was looking down raptly into a broad, natural bowl. She was not crying.

She might well have cried.

In that bowl were thousands upon thousands of dead. On the lips of each decedent was the blue-white frost of *ice-nine*.

Since the corpses were not scattered or tumbled about, it was clear that they had been assembled since the withdrawal of the frightful winds. And, since each corpse had its finger in or near its mouth, I understood that each person had delivered himself to this melancholy place and then poisoned himself with *ice-nine*.

There were men, women, and children, too, many in the attitudes of *boko-maru*. All faced the centre of the bowl, as though they were spectators in an amphitheatre.

Mona and I looked at the focus of all those frosted eyes, looked at the centre of the bowl. There was a round clearing there, a place in which one orator might have stood.

Mona and I approached the clearing gingerly, avoiding the morbid statuary. We found a boulder in it. And under the boulder was a pencilled note which said:

To whom it may concern: These people around you are almost all of the survivors on San Lorenzo of the winds that followed the freezing of the sea. These people made a captive of the spurious holy man named Bokonon. They brought him here, placed him at their centre, and commanded him to tell them exactly what God Almighty was up to and what they should now do. The mountebank told them that God was surely trying to kill them, possibly because He was through with them, and that they should have the good manners to die. This, as you can see, they did.

The note was signed by Bokonon.

## 121 *I Am Slow to Answer*

'What a cynic!' I gasped. I looked up from the note and gazed around the death-filled bowl. 'Is *he* here somewhere?'

'I do not see him,' said Mona mildly. She wasn't depressed or angry. In fact, she seemed to verge on laughter. 'He always said he would never take his own advice, because he knew it was worthless.'

'He'd *better* be here!' I said bitterly. 'Think of the gall of the man, advising all these people to kill themselves!'

Now Mona did laugh. I had never heard her laugh. Her laugh was startlingly deep and raw.

'This strikes you as *funny*?'

She raised her arms lazily. 'It's all so simple, that's all. It solves so much for so many, so simply.'

And she went strolling up among the petrified thousands, still laughing. She paused about midway up the slope and faced me. She called down to me, 'Would you wish any of these alive again, if you could? Answer me quickly.

'Not quick enough with your answer,' she called playfully, after half a minute had passed. And, still laughing a little, she touched her finger to the ground, straightened up, and touched the finger to her lips and died.

Did I weep? They say I did. H. Lowe Crosby and his Hazel and little Newton Hoenikker came upon me as I stumbled down the road. They were in Bolivar's one taxicab, which had been spared by the storm. They tell me I was crying. Hazel cried, too, for joy that I was alive.

They coaxed me into the cab.

Hazel put her arm around me. 'You're with your mom, now. Don't you worry about a thing.'

I let my mind go blank. I closed my eyes. It was with deep, idiotic relief that I leaned on that fleshy, humid, barn-yard fool.

## 122 *The Swiss Family Robinson*

They took me to what was left of Franklin Hoenikker's house at the head of the waterfall. What remained was the cave under the waterfall, which had become a sort of igloo under a translucent, blue-white dome of *ice-nine*.

The ménage consisted of Frank, little Newt, and the Crosbys. They had survived in a dungeon in the palace, one far shallower and more unpleasant than the oubliette. They had moved out the moment the winds had abated, while Mona and I had stayed underground for another three days.

As it happened, they had found the miraculous taxicab waiting for them under the arch of the palace gate. They had found a can of white paint, and on the front doors of the cab Frank had painted white stars, and on the roof he had painted the letters of a *granfalloon*: U.S.A.

'And you left the paint under the arch,' I said.

'How did you know?' asked Crosby.

'Somebody else came along and wrote a poem.'

I did not inquire at once as to how Angela Hoenikker Conners and Philip and Julian Castle had met their ends, for I would have had to speak at once about Mona. I wasn't ready to do that yet.

I particularly didn't want to discuss the death of Mona since, as we rode along in the taxi, the Crosbys and little Newt seemed so inappropriately gay.

Hazel gave me a clue to the gaiety. 'Wait until you see how we live. We've got all kinds of good things to eat. Whenever we want water, we just build a campfire and melt some. The Swiss Family Robinson – that's what we call ourselves.'

## 123  Of Mice and Men

A curious six months followed – the six months in which I wrote this book. Hazel spoke accurately when she called our little society the Swiss Family Robinson, for we had survived a storm, were isolated, and the living became very easy indeed. It was not without a certain Walt Disney charm.

No plants or animals survived, it's true. But *ice-nine* preserved pigs and cows and little deer and windrows of birds and berries until we were ready to thaw and cook them. Moreover, there were tons of canned goods to be had for the grubbing in the ruins of Bolivar. And we seemed to be the only people left on San Lorenzo.

Food was no problem, and neither were clothing or shelter, for the weather was uniformly dry and dead and hot. Our health was monotonously good. Apparently all the germs were dead, too – or napping.

Our adjustment became so satisfactory, so complacent, that no one marvelled or protested when Hazel said, 'One good thing anyway, no mosquitoes.'

She was sitting on a three-legged stool in the clearing where Frank's house had stood. She was sewing strips of red, white, and blue cloth together. Like Betsy Ross, she was making an American flag. No one was unkind enough to point out to her that the red was really a peach, that the blue was nearly a Kelly green, and that the fifty stars she had cut out were six-pointed stars of David rather than five-pointed American stars.

Her husband, who had always been a pretty good cook, now simmered a stew in an iron pot over a wood fire nearby. He did all our cooking for us; he loved to cook.

'Looks good, smells good,' I commented.

He winked. 'Don't shoot the cook. He's doing the best he can.'

In the background of this cosy conversation were the nagging dah-dah-dahs and dit-dit-dits of an automatic SOS transmitter Frank had made. It called for help both night and day.

'Save our soullllls,' Hazel intoned, singing along with the transmitter as she sewed, 'save our soullllls.'

'How's the writing going?' Hazel asked me.

'Fine, Mom, just fine.'

'When you going to show us some of it?'

'When it's ready, Mom, when it's ready.'

'A lot of famous writers were Hoosiers.'

'I know.'

'You'll be one of a long, long line.' She smiled hopefully. 'Is it a funny book?'

'I hope so, Mom.'

'I like a good laugh.'

'I know you do.'

'Each person here has some speciality, something to give the rest. You write books that make us laugh, and Frank does science things, and little Newt – he paints pictures for us all, and I sew, and Lowie cooks.'

'"Many hands make much work light." Old Chinese proverb.'

'They were smart in a lot of ways, those Chinese were.'

'Yes, let's keep their memory alive.'

'I wish now I'd studied them more.'

'Well, it was hard to do, even under ideal conditions.'

'I wish now I'd studied everything more.'

'We've all got regrets, Mom.'

'No use crying over spilt milk.'

'As the poet said, Mom, "Of all the words of mice and men, the saddest are, 'It might have been.'"'

'That's so beautiful, and so true.'

## 124 Frank's Ant Farm

I hated to see Hazel finishing the flag, because I was all balled up in her addled plans for it. She had the idea that I had agreed to plant the fool thing on the peak of Mount McCabe.

'If Lowe and I were younger, we'd do it ourselves. Now all we can do is give you the flag and send our best wishes with you.'

'Mom, I wonder if that's really a good place for the flag.'

'What other place *is* there?'

'I'll put on my thinking cap.' I excused myself and went down into the cave to see what Frank was up to.

He was up to nothing new. He was watching an ant farm he had constructed. He had dug up a few surviving ants in the three-dimensional world of the ruins of Bolivar, and he had reduced the dimensions to two by making a dirt and ant sandwich between two sheets of glass. The ants could do nothing without Frank's catching them at it and commenting upon it.

The experiment had solved in short order the mystery of how ants could survive in a waterless world. As far as I know, they were the only insects that did survive, and they did it by forming with their bodies tight balls around grains of *ice-nine*. They would generate enough heat at the centre to kill half their number and produce one bead of dew. The dew was drinkable. The corpses edible.

'Eat, drink, and be merry, for tomorrow we die,' I said to Frank and his tiny cannibals.

His response was always the same. It was a peevish lecture on all the things that people could learn from ants.

My responses were ritualized, too. 'Nature's a wonderful thing, Frank. Nature's a wonderful thing.'

'You know why ants are so successful?' he asked me for the thousandth time. 'They co-*op*-er-ate.'

'That's a hell of a good word – cooperation.'

'Who *taught* them how to make water?'

'Who taught *me* how to make water?'

'That's a silly answer and you know it.'

'Sorry.'

'There was a time when I took people's silly answers seriously. I'm past that now.'

'A milestone.'

'I've grown up a good deal.'

'At a certain amount of expense to the world.' I could say things like that to Frank with an absolute assurance that he would not hear them.

'There was a time when people could bluff me without much trouble because I didn't have much self-confidence in myself.'

'The mere cutting down of the number of people on earth would go a long way to alleviating your own particular social problems,' I suggested. Again, I made the suggestion to a deaf man.

'You *tell* me, you *tell* me who told these ants how to make water,' he challenged me again.

Several times I had offered the obvious notion that God had taught them. And I knew from onerous experience that he would neither reject nor accept this theory. He simply got madder and madder, putting the question again and again.

I walked away from Frank, just as *The Books of Bokonon* advised me to do. 'Beware of the man who works hard to learn something, learns it, and finds himself no wiser than before,' Bokonon tells us. 'He is full of murderous resentment of people who are ignorant without having come by their ignorance the hard way.'

I went looking for our painter, for little Newt.

## 125 The Tasmanians

When I found little Newt, painting a blasted landscape a quarter of a mile from the cave, he asked me if I would drive him into Bolivar to forage for paints. He couldn't drive himself. He couldn't reach the pedals.

So off we went, and, on the way, I asked him if he had any sex urge left. I mourned that I had none – no dreams in that line, nothing.

'I used to dream of women twenty, thirty, forty feet tall,' he told me. 'But now? God, I can't even remember what my Ukrainian midget looked like.'

I recalled a thing I had read about the aboriginal Tasmanians, habitually naked persons who, when encountered by white men in the seventeenth century, were strangers to agriculture, animal husbandry, architecture of any sort, and possibly even fire. They were so contemptible in the eyes of white men, by reason of their ignorance, that they were hunted for sport by the first settlers, who were convicts from England. And the

aborigines found life so unattractive that they gave up repro-
ducing.

I suggested to Newt now that it was a similar hopelessness
that had unmanned us.

Newt made a shrewd observation. 'I guess all the excitement
in bed had more to do with excitement about keeping the
human race going than anybody ever imagined.'

'Of course, if we had a woman of breeding age among us,
that might change the situation radically. Poor old Hazel is
years beyond having even a Mongolian idiot.'

Newt revealed that he knew quite a bit about Mongolian
idiots. He had once attended a special school for grotesque
children, and several of his schoolmates had been Mongoloids.
'The best writer in our class was a Mongoloid named Myrna –
I mean penmanship, not what she actually wrote down. God,
I haven't thought about her for years.'

'Was it a good school?'

'All I remember is what the headmaster used to say all the
time. He was always bawling us out over the loudspeaker
system for some mess we'd made, and he always started out
the same way: "I am sick and tired . . ."'

'That comes pretty close to describing how I feel most of the
time.'

'Maybe that's the way you're supposed to feel.'

'You talk like a Bokononist, Newt.'

'Why shouldn't I? As far as I know, Bokononism is the only
religion that has any commentary on midgets.'

When I hadn't been writing, I'd been poring over *The Books
of Bokonon*, but the reference to midgets had escaped me. I was
grateful to Newt for calling it to my attention, for the quotation
captured in a couplet the cruel paradox of Bokononist thought,
the heartbreaking necessity of lying about reality, and the heartbreaking impossibility of lying about it.

Midget, midget, midget, how he struts and winks,
For he knows a man's as big as what he hopes and thinks!

## 126 Soft Pipes, Play On

'Such a *depressing* religion!' I cried. I directed our conversation
into the area of Utopias, of what might have been, of what should
have been, of what might yet be, if the world would thaw.

But Bokonon had been there, too, had written a whole book
about Utopias, *The Seventh Book*, which he called 'Bokonon's
Republic'. In that book are these ghastly aphorisms:

The hand that stocks the drug stores rules the world.
Let us start our Republic with a chain of drug stores, a chain of
grocery stores, a chain of gas chambers, and a national game. After
that, we can write our Constitution.

I called Bokonon a jigaboo bastard, and I changed the subject
again. I spoke of meaningful, individual heroic acts. I praised in
particular the way in which Julian Castle and his son had chosen
to die. While the tornadoes still raged, they had set out on foot
for the House of Hope and Mercy in the Jungle to give whatever
hope and mercy was theirs to give. And I saw magnificence in
the way poor Angela had died, too. She had picked up a clarinet
in the ruins of Bolivar and had begun to play it at once, without
concerning herself as to whether the mouthpiece might be
contaminated with *ice-nine*.

'Soft pipes, play on,' I murmured huskily.

'Well, maybe you can find some neat way to die, too,' said
Newt.

It was a Bokononist thing to say.

I blurted out my dream of climbing Mount McCabe with some magnificent symbol and planting it there. I took my hands from the wheel for an instant to show him how empty of symbols they were. 'But what in hell would the right symbol *be*, Newt? What in hell would it *be*?' I grabbed the wheel again. 'Here it is, the end of the world; and here I am, almost the very last man; and there it is, the highest mountain in sight. I know now what my *karass* has been up to, Newt. It's been working night and day for maybe half a million years to get me up that mountain.' I wagged my head and nearly wept. 'But what, for the love of God, is supposed to be in my hands?'

I looked out of the car window blindly as I asked that, so blindly that I went more than a mile before realizing that I had looked into the eyes of an old Negro man, a living coloured man, who was sitting by the side of the road.

And then I slowed down. And then I stopped. I covered my eyes.

'What's the matter?' asked Newt.

'I saw Bokonon back there.'

## 127  *The End*

He was sitting on a rock. He was barefoot. His feet were frosty with *ice-nine*. His only garment was a white bedspread with blue tufts. The tufts said Casa Mona. He took no note of our arrival. In one hand was a pencil. In the other was paper.

'Bokonon?'

'Yes?'

'May I ask what you're thinking?'

'I am thinking, young man, about the final sentence for *The Books of Bokonon*. The time for the final sentence has come.'

# PENGUIN ESSENTIALS

---

**EVA LUNA/ISABEL ALLENDE**

'My name is Eva, which means "life", according to a book of names my mother consulted. I was born in the back room of a shadowy house, and grew up amidst ancient furniture, books in Latin, and human mummies, but none of those things made me melancholy, because I came into the world with a breath of the jungle in my memory.'

Isabel Allende tells the sweet and sinister story of an orphan who beguiles the world with her astonishing visions, triumphing over the worst of adversity and bringing light to a dark place.

'A heartfelt novel, powerful enough to make a dictator cry' *Evening Standard*

**OUT OF AFRICA/KAREN BLIXEN**

'I had a farm in Africa, at the foot of the Ngong Hills . . . Up in this high air you breathed easily . . . you woke up in the morning and thought: Here I am, where I ought to be.'

From the moment Karen Blixen arrived in Kenya in 1914 to manage a coffee plantation, her heart belonged to Africa. Drawn to the intense colours and ravishing landscapes, Blixen spent her happiest years on the farm, and her experiences and friendships with the people around her are vividly recalled in these memoirs.

Out of Africa is the story of a remarkable and unconventional woman, and of a way of life that has vanished for ever.

'A compelling story of passion and a movingly poetic tribute to a lost land' *The Times*

---

# PENGUIN ESSENTIALS

### A CLOCKWORK ORANGE/ANTHONY BURGESS

**'What we were after was lashings of ultraviolence'**

In this nightmare vision of youth in revolt, fifteen-year-old Alex and his friends set out on a diabolical orgy of robbery, rape, torture and murder. Alex is jailed for his teenage delinquency and the State tries to reform him – but at what cost?

Social prophecy? Black comedy? Study of freewill? *A Clockwork Orange* is all of these. It is also a dazzling experiment in language, as Burgess creates a new language – 'nadsat', the teenage slang of a not-too-distant future.

'A gruesomely witty cautionary tale' *Time*

### BREAKFAST AT TIFFANY'S/TRUMAN CAPOTE

**'What I've found does the most good is just to get into a taxi and go to Tiffany's. It calms me down right away, the quietness and the proud look of it; nothing very bad could happen to you there, not with those kind men in their nice suits…'**

Meet Holly Golightly – a free spirited, lop-sided romantic girl about town. With her tousled blond hair and upturned nose, dark glasses and chic black dresses, Holly is a style sensation wherever she goes. Her apartment rocks to Martini-soaked parties and she plays hostess to millionaires and gangsters alike. Yet Holly never loses sight of her ultimate dream – to find a real life place like Tiffany's that makes her feel at home.

Full of sharp wit and exuberant, larger-than-life characters which vividly capture the restless, madcap era of 1940s New York, *Breakfast at Tiffany's* will make you fall in love, perhaps for the first time, with a book.

'The most romantic story ever written' Alex James, *Guardian*

# PENGUIN ESSENTIALS

**MY FAMILY AND OTHER ANIMALS/GERALD DURRELL**

**'What we all need,' said Larry, 'is sunshine…a country where we can *grow*.'**

**'Yes, dear, that would be nice,' agreed Mother, not really listening.**

**'I had a letter from George this morning – he says Corfu's wonderful. Why don't we pack up and go to Greece?'**

**'Very well, dear, if you like,' said Mother unguardedly.**

Escaping the ills of the British climate, the Durrell family – acne-ridden Margo, gun-toting Leslie, bookworm Lawrence and budding naturalist Gerry, along with their long suffering mother and Roger the dog – take off for the island of Corfu. But the Durrells find that, reluctantly, they must share their various villas with a menagerie of local fauna – among them scorpions, geckos, toads, bats and butterflies.

Recounted with immense humour and charm *My Family and Other Animals* is a wonderful account of a rare, magical childhood.

'A bewitching book' *Sunday Times*

**THE GREAT GATSBY/F. SCOTT FITZGERALD**

**'There was music from my neighbour's house through the summer nights. In his blue gardens men and girls came and went like moths among the whisperings and the champagne and the stars.'**

Everybody who is anybody is seen at the glittering parties held in millionaire Jay Gatsby's mansion in West Egg, east of New York. The riotous throng congregates in his sumptuous garden, coolly debating Gatsby's origins and mysterious past. None of the frivolous socialites understands him and among various rumours is the conviction that 'he killed a man'. A detached onlooker, Gatsby is oblivious to the speculation he creates, but always seems to be watching and waiting, though no one knows what for.

As the tragic story unfolds, Gatsby's destructive dreams and passions are revealed, leading to disturbing consequences. A brilliant evocation of 1920s high society, *The Great Gatsby* peels away the layers of this glamorous world to display the coldness and cruelty at its heart.

'Not only a page-turner and a heartbreaker, it's one of the most quintessentially American novels ever written' *Time*

# PENGUIN ESSENTIALS

**CAT'S CRADLE/KURT VONNEGUT**

**'All of the true things I am about to tell you are shameless lies.'**

Dr Felix Hoenikker, one of the founding fathers of the atomic bomb, has left a deadly legacy to the world. For he is the inventor of Ice-nine, a lethal chemical capable of freezing the entire planet. The search for its whereabouts leads to Hoenikker's three eccentric children, to a crazed dictator in the Caribbean, to madness.

Will Felix Hoenikker's death wish come true? Will his last, fatal gift to humankind bring about the end that, for all of us, is nigh?

Told with deadpan humour and bitter irony, Kurt Vonnegut's cult tale of global apocalypse preys on our deepest fears of witnessing the end and, worse still, surviving it . . .

'One of the warmest, wisest, funniest voices to be found anywhere in fiction' *Daily Telegraph*

**BRIDESHEAD REVISITED/EVELYN WAUGH**

**'I knew Sebastian by sight long before I met him. That was unavoidable for, from his first week, he was the most conspicuous man of his year by reason of his beauty, which was arresting, and his eccentricities of behaviour, which seemed to know no bounds.'**

Charles Ryder, a lonely student at Oxford, is captivated by the outrageous and exquisitely beautiful Sebastian Flyte. Invited to Brideshead, Sebastian's magnificent family home, Charles welcomes the attentions of its eccentric, aristocratic inhabitants. But he also discovers a world where duty and desire, faith and earthly happiness are in conflict; a world which threatens to destroy his beloved Sebastian.

A scintillating depiction of the decadent, privileged aristocracy prior to the Second World War, *Brideshead Revisited* is widely regarded as Evelyn Waugh's finest work.

'A wildly entertaining, swooningly funny-sad story' *Time*

# PENGUIN ESSENTIALS

**COLD COMFORT FARM/STELLA GIBBONS**

**'We are not like other folk, maybe, but there have always been Starkadders at Cold Comfort Farm...'**

Sensible, sophisticated Flora Poste has been expensively educated to do everything but earn a living. When she is orphaned at twenty, she decides her only option is to descend on relatives – the doomed Starkadders at the aptly named Cold Comfort Farm. There is Judith in a scarlet shawl, heaving with remorse for an unspoken wickedness; raving old Ada Doom, who once saw something nasty in the woodshed; lustful Seth and despairing Reuben, Judith's two sons; and there is Amos, preaching fire and damnation to one and all. As the sukebind flowers, Flora takes each of the family in hand and brings order to their chaos.

*Cold Comfort Farm* is a sharp and clever parody of the melodramatic and rural novel.

'Very probably the funniest book ever written' *Sunday Times*

**GOODBYE TO ALL THAT/ROBERT GRAVES**

**'There has been a lot of fighting hereabouts. The trenches have made themselves rather than been made, and run inconsequently in and out of the big thirty-foot high stacks of bricks; it is most confusing. The parapet of a trench which we don't occupy is built up with ammunition boxes and corpses . . .'**

In one of the most honest and candid self-portraits ever committed to paper, Robert Graves tells the extraordinary story of his experiences as a young officer in the First World War. He describes life in the trenches in vivid, raw detail, how the dehumanizing horrors he witnessed left him shell-shocked. They were to haunt him for the rest of his life.

'One of the classic accounts of the Western Front' *The Times*

# PENGUIN ESSENTIALS

**STEPPENWOLF/HERMANN HESSE**

'The unhappiness that I need and long for . . . is of the kind that will let me suffer with eagerness and die with lust. That is the unhappiness, or happiness, that I am waiting for.'

Alienated from society, Harry Haller is the Steppenwolf, wild, strange and shy. His despair and desire for death draw him into an enchanted, Faustian underworld. Through a series of shadowy encounters – romantic, freakish and savage by turn – Haller begins to rediscover the lost dreams of his youth.

Adopted by the Sixties counterculture, *Steppenwolf* captured the mood of a disaffected generation that was beginning to question everything.

'The gripping and fascinating story of disease in a man's soul, and a savage indictment of bourgeois society' *New York Times*

**LOLITA/VLADIMIR NABOKOV**

'Lolita, light of my life, fire of my loins. My sin, my soul. Lo-lee-ta: the tip of my tongue taking a trip of three steps down the palate to tap, at three, on the teeth. Lo. Lee. Ta.'

Humbert Humbert is a middle-aged, frustrated college professor. In love with his landlady's twelve-year-old daughter Lolita, he'll do anything to possess her. Unable and unwilling to stop himself, he is prepared to commit any crime to get what he wants.

Is he in love or insane? A silver-tongued poet or a pervert? A tortured soul or a monster? Or is he all of these?

'You read Lolita sprawling limply in your chair, ravished, overcome, nodding scandalized assent' Martin Amis, *Observer*

# PENGUIN ESSENTIALS

---

## ON THE ROAD/JACK KEROUAC

'What's your road, man? — holyboy road, madman road, rainbow road, guppy road, any road. It's an anywhere road for anybody anyhow.'

Sal Paradise, young and innocent, joins the slightly crazed Dean Moriarty on a breathless, exuberant ride back and forth across the United States. Their hedonistic search for release or fulfilment through drink, sex, drugs and jazz becomes an exploration of personal freedom, a test of the limits of the American Dream.

A brilliant blend of fiction and autobiography, Jack Kerouac's exhilarating novel defined the new 'Beat' generation and became the bible of the counter culture.

'Pop writing at its best. It changed the way I saw the world, making me yearn for fresh experience' Hanif Kureishi, *Independent on Sunday*

## LADY CHATTERLEY'S LOVER/D.H. LAWRENCE

'Connie was aware, however, of a growing restlessness ... It thrilled inside her body, in her womb, somewhere, till she felt she must jump into water and swim to get away from it; a mad restlessness. It made her heart beat violently for no reason ...'

Lady Constance Chatterley is trapped in a loveless marriage to a man who is impotent. Oppressed by her dreary life, she is drawn to Mellors the gamekeeper. Breaking out against the constraints of society she yields to her instinctive desire for him and discovers the transforming power of physical love which leads them both towards fulfilment.

Banned for many years for its frank depiction of sex, *Lady Chatterley's Lover* was first published by Penguin in 1960 and was at the centre of a sensational obscenity trial at the Old Bailey. D. H. Lawrence himself called it 'the most improper novel in the world'.

'No one ever wrote better about the power struggles of sex and love' Doris Lessing

---

# PENGUIN ESSENTIALS

## WIDE SARGASSO SEA/JEAN RHYS

**'There is no looking glass here and I don't know what I am like now… Now they have taken everything away. What am I doing in this place and who am I?'**

If Antoinette Cosway, a spirited Creole heiress, could have foreseen the terrible future that awaited her, she would not have married the young Englishman. Initially drawn to her beauty and sensuality, he becomes increasingly frustrated by his inability to reach into her soul. He forces Antoinette to conform to his rigid Victorian ideals, unaware that in taking away her identity he is destroying a part of himself as well as pushing her towards madness.

Set against the lush backdrop of 1830s Jamaica, Jean Rhys's powerful, haunting masterpiece was inspired by her fascination with the first Mrs Rochester, the mad wife in Charlotte Brontë's *Jane Eyre*.

'Compelling, painful and exquisite' *Guardian*

## HELL'S ANGELS/HUNTER S. THOMPSON

**'A phalanx of motorcycles came roaring over the hill from the west… the noise was like a landslide, or a wing of bombers passing over. Even knowing the Angels I couldn't quite handle what I was seeing. It was like Genghis Khan, Morgan's Raiders, the Wild One and the Rape of Nanking all at once.'**

In September, 1964 a cavalcade of motorbikes ripped through the city of Monterey, California. It was a trip destined to make Hell's Angels household names across America, infamous for their violent, drunken rampages and feared for the destruction left in their wake.

Enter Hunter S. Thompson, the master of counter-culture journalism who alone had the ability and stature to ride with the Angels on their terms. In this brilliant and hair-raising expose, he journeys with the last outlaws of the American frontier.

A mixture of journalism, story-telling and sheer bravado, *Hell's Angels* is Hunter S. Thompson at full throttle.

'The maverick voice of American counterculture' *Guardian*

# PENGUIN ESSENTIALS

---

**BONJOUR TRISTESSE/FRANÇOISE SAGAN**

'**Late into the night we talked of love, of its complications. In my father's eyes they were imaginary. . . This conception of rapid, violent and passing love affairs appealed to my imagination. I was not at the age when fidelity is attractive. I knew very little about love.**'

The French Riviera: home to the Beautiful People. And none are more beautiful than Cécile, a precocious seventeen-year-old, and her father Raymond, a vivacious libertine. Charming, decadent and irresponsible, the golden-skinned duo are dedicated to a life of free love, fast cars and hedonistic pleasures. But then, one long, hot summer Raymond decides to marry, and Cécile and her lover Cyril feel compelled to take a hand in his amours, with tragic consequences.

*Bonjour Tristesse* scandalized 1950s France with its portrayal of teenager *terrible* Cécile, a heroine who rejects conventional notions of love, marriage and responsibility to choose her own sexual freedom.

'A funny, thoroughly immoral and thoroughly French tale' *The Times*

**A CONFEDERACY OF DUNCES/JOHN KENNEDY TOOLE**

'**This city is famous for its gamblers, prostitutes, exhibitionists, anti-Christs, alcoholics, sodomites, drug addicts, fetishists, onanists, pornographers, frauds, jades, litterbugs, and lesbians . . . don't make the mistake of bothering *me*.**'

Ignatius J. Reilly: fat, flatulent, eloquent and almost unemployable. By the standards of ordinary folk he is pretty much unhinged, too. But is he bothered by this?

No. For this misanthropic crusader against an America fallen into vice and ignorance has a mission: to rescue a naked female philosopher in distress. And he has a pirate costume and hot-dog cart to do it with . . .

'A fine funny novel. This is the kind of book one wants to keep quoting from' Anthony Burgess

---

# PENGUIN ESSENTIALS

The Penguin Essentials are some of the twentieth-century's most important books. When they were first published they changed the way we thought about literature and about life. And they have remained vital reading ever since. These new, stylish editions remind readers that once upon a time each book in the Essentials series was the only book worth being seen with.

Eva Luna by Isabel Allende

Out of Africa by Karen Blixen

A Clockwork Orange by Anthony Burgess

Breakfast at Tiffany's by Truman Capote

My Family and Other Animals by Gerald Durrell

The Great Gatsby by F. Scott Fitzgerald

A Room with a View by E.M. Forster

Cold Comfort Farm by Stella Gibbons

Goodbye to All That by Robert Graves

Steppenwolf by Hermann Hesse

On the Road by Jack Kerouac

Lady Chatterley's Lover by D.H. Lawrence

Lolita by Vladimir Nabokov

Wide Sargasso Sea by Jean Rhys

Bonjour Tristesse by Françoise Sagan

Hell's Angels by Hunter S. Thompson

A Confederacy of Dunces by John Kennedy Toole

Cat's Cradle by Kurt Vonnegut

Brideshead Revisited by Evelyn Waugh